"The B and B's on fire."

Luke tried the front door. Locked.

He raced to the back of the house, tried the knob and was ready to crash through when he raised his eyes.

A woman stood in the second-story window, frantically pounding her hands against the glass.

Climbing onto the porch railing, Luke shimmied up the column, then hoisted himself onto the ledge. Reaching the window, he pounded on the glass.

"Move back," he warned. She stepped aside, and Luke twisted his jacket around his hand, raised his fist and shattered the glass.

He grabbed the woman and guided her to the windowsill.

"I've got you. We jump on three. One. Two. Three."

They jumped just before the room exploded, spewing a ball of fire into the night.

Books by Debby Giusti

Love Inspired Suspense

Nowhere to Hide
Scared to Death
MIA: Missing in Atlanta
*Countdown to Death

*Magnolia Medical

DEBBY GIUSTI

is a medical technologist who loves working with test tubes and petri dishes almost as much as she loves to write. Growing up as an army brat, Debby met and married her husband—then a captain in the army—at Fort Knox, Kentucky. Together they traveled the world, raised three wonderful army brats of their own and have now settled in Atlanta, Georgia, where Debby spins tales of suspense that touch the heart and soul.

Contact Debby through her Web site, www.DebbyGiusti.com, e-mail debby@debbygiusti.com or write c/o Steeple Hill Books, 233 Broadway, Suite 1001, New York, NY 10279.

Debby Giusti
Countdown
to
Death

Steeple
Hill®

Published by Steeple Hill Books™

STEEPLE HILL BOOKS

Steeple
Hill®

ISBN-13: 978-0-373-44310-9
ISBN-10:   0-373-44310-2

COUNTDOWN TO DEATH

Copyright © 2008 by Deborah W. Giusti

www.SteepleHill.com

Printed in U.S.A.

May your kindness, O Lord, be upon us
who have put our hope in you.
—Psalms 33:22

To all medical laboratory professionals,
especially my former coworkers at
Peachtree Regional Hospital

To Tony, Liz, Joe, Mary, Katie and Eric
Your love and support mean so much to me

To Darlene, Annie and Anna

To Emily Rodmell, Jessica Alvarez
and Deidre Knight

Thank you!

ONE

Allison Stewart's future hung in the balance. Her job. Her research. Her attempt to make a difference.

Two years working on a new laboratory test to detect blood-borne pathogens, and the board still couldn't decide if she deserved additional funding.

Pulling in a calming breath, she slipped her hands into the powdered latex gloves and snipped off a segment of tubing from three units of blood.

Collected at a South Georgia blood draw earlier in the week, the units had been transported to Magnolia Medical's laboratory in Atlanta for processing. Ensuring the blood was safe for transfusion was top priority.

The units had passed the routine battery of tests.

They'd flunked Allison's.

She spun the segments in the centrifuge, then transferred the top layer of golden serum into the analyzer.

The test was a semiautomated procedure. Rapid, if not reliable.

Given time, she'd work out the kinks.

The instrumentation clicked into operation.

If she believed in the power of prayer, this would be the time to ask for help. But God had turned His back on her years ago. No reason anything would change today.

Discarding her gloves, she wiped her damp palms against the side of her lab coat. Behind her, footsteps sounded across the polished tile floor. She turned as Veronica Edwards, the research department's laboratory manager, entered the special projects area.

"I thought you'd be tied up all afternoon with the directors." Allison noted her supervisor's drawn face and furrowed brow. Evidently, the meeting hadn't gone well.

"The board cut your funding."

Allison's chest tightened. "Did you tell them I'm optimistic about perfecting the procedure?"

"They're focused on cost reduction, not sinking more money into a laboratory test that, with time, *may* detect a rare prion disease."

"A rare but fatal prion disease," Allison corrected her.

"Which has never posed a significant problem in the U.S."

The muscles in Allison's neck tensed. "Great Britain didn't think it had a problem until the prion outbreak there. Remember the havoc mad cow disease caused? We're still restricting donations from people who lived in Europe during that time for fear *they* will infect *our* blood supply."

Veronica sighed. "I understand the significance of your research. If we can find a way to identify the dormant prion protein, we can lift the European restriction."

"And end the blood-shortage crisis. Magnolia Medical would control the patent on a test sure to be adopted in every blood-donor center throughout the country. The revenue alone would—"

"But two years with no hint of success, Allison. It's over."

The analyzer stopped. Thirty seconds and the results would feed to the monitor.

Time to come clean. Her supervisor needed to be brought up to date.

"I ran random specimens yesterday from that last blood draw, expecting the units to be negative. Three reacted so I tested them again this morning with the same results." Allison tried to smile but knew she fell short. "They say the third time's a charm. I repeated the procedure just now."

Allison glanced at the monitor as the results rolled across the screen. "The levels are identical to the first two runs."

"Meaning?"

"Meaning three donors will soon develop neurological symptoms that will eventually lead to death."

Veronica stepped closer. "The likelihood of

picking up a single positive specimen—let alone three—in one blood draw is—" her eyes widened "—unheard of."

"We never had a rapid, cost-effective test to screen donor blood before."

Veronica held up her index finger. "A test that's still in the experimental phase."

Do or die. Allison was gambling everything on the next bit of information she needed to share.

"The three positive specimens came from donors who live in the same small town—Sterling, Georgia."

The lab manager's eyebrow shot up. "You accessed their personal donor data?"

Allison nodded. "According to the information I found online, the area is a haven for deer hunters. Maybe the men ate venison from deer with chronic wasting disease. I'll drive to Sterling after work tonight. If I talk to the men, I may find a common link."

Veronica shook her head. "I don't like it."

"Three days and I should have an answer."

Veronica caved. "Two days. But watch what you say. I wouldn't want anyone to be told they have a fatal disease because of a questionable result from a test that's far from ready for clinical use. And no contact with the media. We don't want any wild stories about an outbreak of mad cow disease in Georgia. Invalid test results would blacken Magnolia Medical's good name."

"But the test *is* valid," Allison said with conviction.

"Then find the connection with infected deer."

Veronica headed for the door, but Allison's next comment caused her to pause. "Venison may not be the source of infection."

Veronica held up her hand. "If you're thinking contaminated beef is the problem, you're jumping to a conclusion I'm not willing to consider. Find the reason for the positive reactions. See whether they tie in with a diseased deer population."

"And if not?" Allison asked.

Neither of them gave voice to the obvious. If the test were valid and if eating or handling contaminated venison had not infected the men, then an even more serious situation was raising its ugly head in South Georgia. A situation that could impact the entire southeast, if not the nation.

"Then God help us," Veronica said as she turned on her heel and left the lab.

After all that had happened, Luke Garrison was riding on empty. His sister's handicap, the trauma that had pushed her farther into a world of isolation, their father's tragic death. Ten years ago, yet the memories were too real, too fresh. Any hope for the future seemed as elusive as the moonbeams filtering through the cloudy night sky.

Luke pulled his eyes from the long stretch of

highway that led back to Sterling and glanced at his sister, Shelly, sleeping in the backseat of his SUV.

"Poor thing, she's worn out," his aunt said from the passenger seat.

"So are you." Luke noted the fatigue that lined the older woman's face. Even her vibrant red hair seemed limp and lifeless in the half-light coming from the dash. "Shelly's trips to the doctor in Atlanta take their toll on you, Bett."

"You worry as much as I do about her. If only the doctor would offer some encouragement."

"We'll keep praying for a miracle," he said, hearing more optimism in his voice than he felt.

A decade of pain remained heavy on his heart.

Letting out a frustrated breath, he forced his gaze back to the road, determined to send the memories scurrying into the night.

The lights from town glowed in the distance.

Bett's eyes began to droop and her head rested on the seat back as she drifted into a light slumber.

At the fork in the road, Luke veered left onto the desolate two-lane that skirted Sterling—the route he had routinely chosen since his father's death. No need to give the townspeople more fuel for their insistent chatter. As far as he was concerned, the less time he spent in town the better.

Up ahead, the old Wallace Bed and Breakfast stood out against the cloudy sky, the only structure on this stretch of lonely back road.

What a shame to let such a beautiful place go so long without upkeep. If repairs weren't done soon, even the few travelers who meandered through Sterling would find lodging elsewhere.

Thank you, Cooper Wallace. So much for greedy lawyers who always thought of the bottom line.

Luke glanced again at the once-stately Victorian. A light flickered in the upstairs hall window. The glass shimmered in the night.

Shimmered like—

Realization hit him full force. *Fire!*

He swerved to the side of the road and slammed on the brakes.

Bett's eyes flew open.

"The B and B's on fire. Call for help!"

Before she could find her cell, Luke was out of the car and running toward the shingled structure.

He tried the front door. Locked.

"Fire! Open up! Everyone out," he screamed, pounding the brass knocker against the thick oak.

Please, God, if anyone's staying the night, let them hear me.

The kitchen entrance might be open.

He raced to the back of the house, tried the doorknob and was ready to crash through the door when he raised his eyes.

A woman stood at the second-story window, frantically pounding her hands against the glass.

Heart in his throat, Luke slammed his full weight

against the kitchen door, relieved when the aged oak gave way. Inside, the smoke rolled through the house, thick and black.

"Fire," he screamed again.

A middle-aged man coughed as he staggered from the darkness.

"How many people are staying here?" Luke asked.

"A guy and his wife are in the back bedroom. They're headed this way. But someone's trapped upstairs. The fire's raging at the top of the staircase. There's no way to reach her."

"Where's the night manager?"

"He left hours ago."

Before the man finished speaking, a young couple stumbled into the kitchen. The woman gasped for air.

"Get outside," Luke ordered. He reached for the woman's arm and guided the three of them to safety.

As they scurried away from the house, Luke looked up once again. An increased sense of dread slipped over him. Unable to break the window, the woman stood outlined against the deadly glow from the fire that filled the room.

Climbing onto the porch railing, Luke shimmied up the column holding the drainage spout to the overhanging roof, then hoisted himself onto the ledge that rimmed the second story.

Adrenaline coursed like lightning through his veins as he scooted toward the window, aware of the growing crackle of the flames coming from within the aged structure. A section of the narrow railing broke. His foot gave way. He grabbed the rough shingles, holding on with his fingertips, and hugged the wall to maintain his balance.

His rapidly beating heart seemed as loud as the sirens wailing through the night. Fire trucks would arrive soon, but not in time to save the woman.

He inched forward. Sweat trickled down his back and dampened his shirt.

Reaching the window, he pounded on the glass.

She turned at the sound, her face wrapped in terror.

"Move back," he warned, shrugging out of his jacket.

Had she heard him?

As if his words had finally registered, she stepped aside and covered her face with her arms.

Luke twisted his jacket around his right hand, raised his fist and jammed it against the window. The pane shattered.

With a series of sweeps, he cleared away the remaining shards of glass.

Fueled by the increased oxygen, the fire burned bright, the roar deafening.

Luke grabbed the woman and guided her over the windowsill. She clung to him, her fingers digging into his flesh.

"I've got you," he assured her. "We jump on three."

She shook her head. "I…I can't."

"You have to," he insisted. "One… Two…"

He wrapped his arm protectively around her waist. "Three."

They jumped just before the room exploded, spewing a ball of fire into the night.

A clump of overgrown azalea bushes broke their fall. Together they rolled and came to rest on a mound of thick pine needles.

Luke groaned as he pulled himself to a sitting position.

Lights flashed. The fire chief appeared, yelling orders to his men. A scurry of activity surrounded them as hoses stretched toward the flames. Water hissed from the nozzles.

The woman lay on the ground, eyes closed, golden hair streaming around a face pale as death.

"Ma'am?" Luke nudged her shoulder. "Ma'am?"

When she didn't respond, he touched her neck. No pulse.

"She needs help," he shouted, hoping to attract attention.

Knowing every second was critical, Luke tilted her head back. With swift, sure movements, he blew two quick puffs of air into her mouth, then, intertwining his fingers, he pressed down on her sternum.

"And one, and two…" He counted the compressions.

Where were the medical personnel?

"And three, and—"

"We'll take it from here." A team of EMTs scurried to his aid.

Luke edged back to let them do their job.

Bett raced toward him. "Someone said you went into the burning building."

"I'm fine," he assured her as he stood and looked around. "Where's Shelly?"

"In the car. Mrs. Rogers heard the sirens and stopped by to help. She's with Shelly. I was worried. They told me you pulled a person from the fire."

He pointed to where the EMTs clustered.

Bett grabbed his arm. "You're hurt, Luke."

For the first time, he noticed the gash on his forearm and the blood that matted his shirt.

"It's a small cut." He shrugged off her concern while his eyes fixed once again on the woman he'd tried to save.

The spotlights cutting through the night, the frantic rush of the emergency personnel and the acrid stench of the smoke took him back, and for a moment he saw Hilary's lifeless body lying on the ground.

A lump filled his throat. *Lord, don't let another woman die.*

Chaos. Allison felt the swell of confusion and panic surround her. She gasped for air.

A mask covered her mouth and nose. She tried to push it aside.

Someone restrained her hand.

"Breathe, lady."

Her chest burned.

"Come on, lady. You gotta breathe."

She pulled in a shallow breath, expecting smoke. Instead her lungs filled with life-giving oxygen. She gulped, sucking in the pure air.

"She's coming 'round," the voice announced. "Tell Luke. Only way he'll calm down is if he knows she's okay."

A few moments later, a hand touched her shoulder.

She blinked open her eyes and saw the man who'd saved her life.

His cheeks were covered with soot. Blood streaked through his thick chestnut hair where he'd wiped his arm across his forehead.

Dark eyes searched her face. "Are you okay?"

"You saved my life," she managed to whisper.

"I thought…" Concern wrinkled his brow. "When you didn't respond, I was worried you wouldn't make it."

She smiled, or at least tried to smile through the oxygen mask.

An EMT tapped his shoulder. "Sorry, Luke, but the county medical van just arrived. The doc wants to examine her."

Before she could say goodbye, the man who'd saved her disappeared into the crowd of onlookers.

To Allison's surprise, the medical van was state-of-the-art and the doctor's exam thorough. Irritated lungs, which improved after the breathing treatments that the EMTs administered, and a strained back were her only injuries.

"You're one lucky lady," the fire chief said to her later as she sat outside the medical van and watched the men roll up their hoses. The front of the house and kitchen had been saved. A gaping black hole was all that remained of the room where she'd been staying.

She refused to think of what might have happened.

"B and B's the only place that rents rooms in this area," the chief continued. "The gentleman who was staying downstairs plans to drive seventy miles to the next town where a motor lodge has vacancies. Younger couple moved in with someone they know in Sterling."

He stared at her, evidently waiting for an answer to a question she never heard him ask.

"Are you telling me I need to find a place to stay?"

"We've got an empty cabin." A middle-aged woman with a weatherworn face, warm eyes and flaming red hair stepped forward from the group lingering close by. "Be happy to offer you lodging for as long as you're in town."

The woman patted Allison's hand. "Bet you're worn-out after everything that's happened. We'll take good care of you, honey."

Hearing the compassion in the older woman's

voice, unexpected tears stung Allison's eyes. She tried to blink them back.

Must be letdown after all that had happened. Either that, or the meds the doctor had given her.

"I thought you folks closed up the cabin." The fire chief rubbed his hand over his chin. "After that boarder of yours—"

"Don't need to focus on the past, Chief." The woman cut him off, her voice sharp. Then she dug in her pocket, pulled out a clean tissue and handed it to Allison.

"The place is neat as a pin and ready for my new friend. My name's Elizabeth Garrison. Folks call me Bett."

Allison blew her nose and tried to smile at the second person who had come to her aid that night. Then, remembering her car, she rummaged in the shoulder bag she'd had the presence of mind to wrap about her neck as soon as she'd smelled smoke.

Keys in hand, she tried to stand and grimaced as the pulled muscles in her back responded to the shift in position.

"I'll take those," a deep voice said behind her.

She turned and looked into her rescuer's eyes.

"Did I overhear my aunt say you're coming home with us?" He took the keys with his left hand and stuck out his right, a thick square of gauze taped to his forearm. "Seems we didn't have time for introductions earlier. I'm Luke Garrison."

She slipped her hand into his, feeling a connection. After all, he'd saved her life.

"Allison Stewart," she mumbled, suddenly light-headed. Probably the medication taking effect.

"I'll drive your car," he said, then glanced at the older woman. "Bett, you take Shelly home in the SUV."

"I hate to impose after all you've done," Allison insisted, not wanting to be a pest.

His lips eased into a smile, but his eyes were serious. "I need to make sure nothing else happens to you tonight."

Bett and Shelly pulled onto the two-lane street, heading home, as Luke settled Allison into the passenger side of her car and slipped into the driver's seat next to her.

The cloud cover broke, exposing a crescent moon and stars twinkling in the sky. Venus, named after the goddess of love, hovered low on the horizon, reminding him of the Greek mythology he'd studied in college. He shook his head ever so slightly. Probably the close proximity of an attractive woman that had him thinking of love.

Or maybe it was due to the sweet floral scent that lingered in her car and contrasted sharply with the acrid smoke that clung to his clothes.

Today's weather report forecast the first October frost, and over the past few hours, the temperature had dropped to near freezing. Luke reached for the heater control and turned to his passenger, still wrapped in a blanket the EMTs had given her. She looked bone-tired.

"Cold?"

She rubbed her arms and nodded. "Maybe a little."

He adjusted the thermostat until warm air flowed from the vents.

"I've got a cell phone, if you'd like to call family to let them know you're okay."

"Mine's in my purse." She patted the small shoulder bag still draped around her neck. "I'll call my laboratory manager tomorrow in case the fire makes the Atlanta news."

"Where do you work?"

"Magnolia Medical. It's a health-care facility. Clinical labs, physical and occupational therapy, that type of thing. I'm in the research branch."

After the endless battery of tests Shelly had been put through, medical personnel didn't rank high on Luke's list of important people. Bett had insisted extended therapy in Atlanta would help. He'd never told his aunt, but he wondered if Shelly's recovery had been delayed because the specialists had pushed her too hard.

"Surely you're not here because of your research?" he asked, surprised by the edge in his voice. "Something to do with the local wildlife?"

She turned to stare at him. "Why do you ask?"

He could see the question in her blue eyes even in the dim reflection of light from the dashboard controls.

"A couple guys were talking while you were being treated by the doc. They said you stopped by the Roadside Grill on your way into town and quizzed the waitress about the wild game on the menu."

"Folks in Sterling like to talk."

"It's a small town." He shrugged. "News travels."

"I didn't expect them to serve venison," she said.

He raised an eyebrow. "PETA or anti-gun?"

"Pardon?"

"Sounds like you're against hunting."

"I never said that."

"But you insinuated it. At least that's what the men led me to believe."

"And you believe everything you hear?"

She had him there.

"Look, I'm sorry," he said.

"And so am I." She pulled her hair back from her face and sighed. "The fact is, I'm working on a laboratory test to ensure the safety of our blood supply. It's in the developmental stage, and I picked up some unexpected results."

"If they have to do with the deer population, you might want to notify the game warden."

"It's a little too early to involve him. At this point, the results of my test are questionable."

"Then you don't think there's a problem with the venison?"

"I don't know what to think."

Neither did he. Allison looked as confused as she sounded.

What had he read about diseases humans could get from deer? He thought of the article he'd written on hunting safety. "Only thing that comes to mind involving infected venison is chronic wasting disease. We've never had a problem in Georgia."

Allison's eyes widened. "I didn't mention the name of the disease."

"No, you didn't. But I wrote an article for a hunting magazine a few months back on the danger of infected game."

She rolled her eyes and groaned. "You're a journalist?"

"Actually I run a manufacturing company and do a little farming on the side. In my spare time, I pen articles for a regional hunting magazine."

"Time-out, okay?" She put one hand over the other to form a *T.* "The doc gave me a muscle relaxer that's making me talk too much. Do me a favor and let's change the subject."

Typical for medical types. Throw out information, then refuse to discuss the situation fully. Shelly's doctors had done the same thing numerous times, causing Luke undue frustration.

Although frustration wasn't what he was feeling tonight. More like concern.

He didn't know a thing about the woman sitting next to him, but he knew about the danger wasting disease posed to hunters. Even if they didn't eat the infected venison, handling the carcass—especially if they had cuts on their hands—could increase the risk of exposure. Yet Allison had admitted her results were questionable.

He made a mental note to call the game warden in the morning. Luke hadn't seen any sickly animals on his property, but it wouldn't hurt to notify the authorities to be on the lookout.

They rode in silence for over a mile until Allison tilted her head back against the seat. "Your aunt seems like a nice lady. What about the rest of your family?"

He shrugged. "Not much to tell. Bett's helping me raise my sister."

"So Shelly's not your daughter?"

The look on her face caused him to chuckle. "Do I look like an old married guy?"

"No, but—" She smiled. "I told you I'm not thinking straight. And your parents?"

"They're both dead."

He heard the finality in his voice, and to her credit, Allison didn't push for more information. Instead, she mumbled a few words of sympathy and closed her eyes.

Pretty, even with the soot that smudged her face.

No matter why she'd come to Sterling, Luke would let her stay in the cabin for a day or two while she tracked down the information she needed. She'd probably be on her way by the end of the week.

Doubtful she'd disrupt his routine in that short time. After all, he'd worked too long to build a protective cocoon where his sister could live without being reminded of the past. Despite the doctors' prognosis, Luke believed Shelly would eventually have a breakthrough. He wouldn't let anything set her back again.

Even an attractive scientist who seemed to need protection herself.

Allison knew when to keep quiet. The tone of Luke's voice had made it clear his parents' deaths were off-limits as a topic of discussion. She understood limits. She'd placed boundaries on her past as well.

Besides, she didn't feel like talking. Her back ached and a heavy weight sat on her chest from the amount of smoke she'd inhaled. Common sense told her she should have followed the doctor's advice and gone to the hospital for observation. But the facility was seventy-five miles away, and she didn't have time to twiddle her thumbs while the doc on duty determined she could be released in the morning.

She needed to find the reason for her test results

before someone in Atlanta decided to release the three units for transfusion.

"It's over, Allison," the laboratory manager's words echoed through her mind.

Allison had worked too long and come too far to have her research dismissed so quickly.

The hum of the tires along the country road, the warmth of the heater and the darkness lulled Allison into a light slumber.

She blinked her eyes open when the car came to a stop in front of a small log cabin with a wide porch, where Luke's aunt waved a greeting. Two wrought-iron lights illuminated a glider swing and rocking chair.

Rounding the car, Luke opened the passenger door and held out his hand. Placing hers in his, she felt the strength of his grasp, grateful for his support as her stiff muscles refused to readily comply.

"Shelly's in bed and waiting for you to tell her good-night," Bett said to Luke, then, wrapping her arm around Allison, she ushered her toward the cabin. "I've got everything ready for you, dear."

"Take good care of her," Luke said as their hands parted.

"Now come on, honey. I'll get you settled." Bett opened the cabin door. Before Allison stepped inside, she glanced back at Luke, who walked purposely toward a large, sprawling farmhouse about fifty yards away.

What was it about Luke Garrison? He'd saved her life, for which she'd be eternally grateful. Both he and his aunt seemed welcoming with their offer of lodging and attention to her needs.

He had seemed friendly enough until she'd mentioned his parents. Death was hard. Something she knew firsthand. Evidently, Luke was a private person who kept his feelings to himself.

But his tone of voice sent a question niggling at the back of her mind.

Was there something he wanted to keep secret about their deaths?

TWO

The next morning, Allison's eyes opened with a start to the gray haze filtering through the calico curtains. Her hand touched the crisp cotton sheet and thick multicolored quilt that covered the bed where she lay.

Her body ached. She stretched to ensure her muscles would respond, then wiggled her fingers and toes. Nothing broken.

Recollection flooded over her. The fire, her cries for help, strong hands that pulled her from the burning building.

Death had almost found her in Sterling, Georgia. Not a good way to start her stay.

Rising in the bed, she grimaced when the muscles in her back protested; she stretched, hoping to ease out the kinks. Once on her feet, she parted the curtain and spied her car parked outside.

Last night seemed a blur. The doctor had given her something to help her relax. Evidently, it had taken effect before she'd arrived at the cabin.

No other motel or hotel in town. Luckily, no one had been hurt in the fire. And the man who had saved her?

She remembered the determination in his voice before they'd jumped. About the only thing she was able to clearly recall.

Brain still as fuzzy as cotton batting, she spied her purse on the nightstand and her overnight bag on the floor.

Slowly the events of the night before unfolded. Once she'd found her room at the B and B, she'd been too tired to retrieve her suitcase from the car. Instead she had dozed on the bed and awakened later, smelling smoke.

Gratitude filled her again.

Luke and his aunt—

What was her name? Bett Garrison. That was it. They'd been so kind to offer lodging.

Allison hadn't expected their generosity or the sense of relief that washed over her now. She could have died in the fire.

A déjà vu of Drew.

She shook off the thought. This wasn't the time or place to revisit the past.

Better to deal with the issue at hand.

Closing the curtain, Allison turned from the window and opened her suitcase. She needed to find the Garrisons to thank them for their hospitality before she headed to town to talk to the men she'd tried to contact by phone yesterday. She'd left two messages on voice mail and had arranged an interview with the only person she could reach at home.

One in three. Not good odds.

Once dressed, Allison stepped outside into the overcast morning and shuffled toward the two-story frame farmhouse, her body refusing to move at any pace but slow. A barn sat in the distance near a rolling pasture where a few head of cattle grazed.

The house had a tin roof, black shutters and a wraparound porch neatly arranged with a rattan love seat, chair and dual rockers. The surrounding hardwood trees—sweet gums, maples and oaks— wore their fall colors, from bright reds to burnt umber. The breeze fluttered through the trees, sending a shower of leaves that piled like giant confetti on the ground below.

The screen door opened and Bett welcomed her with a wide smile. Her red hair was pulled into a clip at the base of her neck. She wore jeans and a pullover sweater and looked rested and fresh.

"I was wondering how late you'd sleep. Breakfast is ready. 'Spect you're hungry after that ordeal last night. I've got eggs, sausage, grits and corn bread waiting on the stove."

"You've been so kind. Thank you, Bett."

"Nice to have company to look after. Gets kind of lonely around here sometimes." She watched as Allison crept up the porch steps. "How's the back?"

"Much better."

Inside, a leather couch and love seat sat in front of a floor-to-ceiling stacked stone fireplace. Hunting magazines lay neatly arranged on the coffee table, and a mounted deer head hung over the mantel. Definitely a man's room.

A second door led to an area off the kitchen where a round oak pedestal table, covered with a linen cloth, was set for four.

"Sit there, dear." Bett pointed to a chair and reached for the coffeepot.

"Luke will be downstairs in a minute. We home-school Shelly, and he's helping her with today's lesson."

"So it's just the three of you?"

"That's right. My brother—Luke's dad—passed away about ten years ago. And Luke's mother died shortly after Shelly was born."

Seems Bett didn't have a problem discussing their deaths. "I'm sorry."

"The Lord knows what He's doing even when we don't understand."

Allison wished she could be half as positive when it came to anything to do with God.

Bett poured coffee into a mug and handed it to Allison. The rich aroma of the fresh brew, mixed with the smell of corn bread and sausage, was making her mouth water. She blew into the hot liquid and took a sip, feeling at ease in the comfortable kitchen.

A door opened behind her. Allison turned, and just that quickly, her sense of serenity vanished, replaced with a nervous tingle that warmed her from the inside out.

Luke stood in the doorway. Lean and lanky with broad shoulders that filled out the plaid shirt tucked into well-worn jeans.

"Come on now, Shelly," he called. "The lady won't hurt you."

Glancing into the kitchen, he flashed a smile at Allison that caused her cheeks to burn.

"Shelly's shy around strangers," he explained.

Which was exactly the way Allison was feeling at the moment.

"How's your back?" he asked.

"Probably better than your arm," she said, returning his smile.

"Then we're both in good shape." Even from across the room, she could see the twinkle in his eyes.

As they spoke, a girl shyly peeked at Allison from the hallway beyond the open door. Slender like her aunt with the same red hair. At first glance, Shelly appeared to be about sixteen, but as she stepped forward, Allison noted her innocent facial expressions and the faraway look in her eyes. Undoubtedly, she was a special child with a mental age much younger than her actual years.

"Go on, now," Luke encouraged, his hand nudging her into the room.

With a reassuring nod from her brother, Shelly shuffled toward the table. She favored her left leg, causing a lateral swing to her gait.

Once she was seated, Luke grabbed her napkin from the table, shook it open and placed it over her lap. "Remember your manners, darlin', and eat like the little lady you are."

Shelly's eyes crinkled, but her mouth refused to smile.

Luke's gaze was warm, and Allison could see the deep affection he had for his sister.

Standing at the stove, Bett fixed a plate and placed it in front of Shelly.

"How 'bout you, Allison? Two links or three?" Bett held the spatula poised above the skillet, where plump sausage sizzled. "Best venison sausage you'll ever eat."

Venison?

Luke flicked a quick glance her way.

"Just eggs, please. No sausage."

Bett handed Allison her plate, then fixed one for Luke and herself before she sat at the table.

Realizing how hungry she really was, Allison picked up her fork ready to dig into the eggs when an awkward silence settled over the room. She looked up to find Luke staring at her.

"Shall we offer thanks?"

Her cheeks burned. "Of course."

She returned the fork to her plate, bowed her

head and clasped her hands together on her lap. Major faux pas. So much for trying to fit in.

Luke spoke in a sincere voice. "Thank you, God, for the food we are about to eat. Thank you for protecting Allison from the fire and for giving us the opportunity to know her better. May we honor you in all we do this day. Amen."

Reaching for his knife and fork, Luke cut Shelly's sausage into bite-size pieces and spread a thick layer of golden butter over her corn bread.

Once again Allison's cheeks burned. "Seems I'm late expressing my thanks."

"Just glad I happened to be driving by."

"If you hadn't—"

He nodded almost imperceptibly toward his sister. Allison understood that Shelly didn't need to hear the reality of what could have happened.

Not that Allison wanted to give voice to that thought, either.

Bett smiled and patted her arm. "No need to dwell on what might have been. We're just thanking the Lord you're here with us today."

Her touch was filled with acceptance. Something Allison had little of from her own family.

"Shelly, after breakfast I want you to help me in the garden. We've got the last of the pole beans to pick before we finish your lessons and then work on our crafts." Bett continued to chatter about the day ahead of them.

Relieved the conversation had turned to other topics, Allison ate heartily. Once finished, she wiped her mouth on the napkin and sighed with satisfaction.

"Breakfast was delicious."

Bett beamed with the compliment and started to clear the table.

"Let me help you with the dishes." Allison rose from the chair just as the doorbell rang.

Luke excused himself and quickly returned, followed by a middle-aged, beefy man dressed in a khaki uniform with a badge on his chest.

"Morning, Bett."

She tucked a strand of hair behind her ear and smiled warmly. "How 'bout some breakfast, Vic?"

"Can I take a rain check?"

"Allison, Sheriff Vic Treadwell wants to talk to us about last night," Luke said.

"Ma'am." The sheriff nodded to Allison, then smiled at Shelly. "Hey, Sunshine."

The girl's eyes crinkled, and the corners of her mouth twitched at the nickname she evidently enjoyed being called.

"Why don't we go into the other room," the sheriff suggested.

A sense of unease washed over Allison. She rinsed her hands in the sink and dried them on the towel Bett offered, then followed Luke and the sheriff into the living area.

Pulling in a steadying breath, she sat on one end

of the leather couch opposite the sheriff, who withdrew a small tablet and pen from his pocket. Luke stood by the mantel.

"Allison, did you happen to hear anything before the fire broke out last night?" the sheriff asked, his pen poised to write.

She shook her head, trying to calm the threads of concern that tangled within her. "The drive from Atlanta took longer than I expected. I called a friend after I found my room and before I'd gotten my luggage from the car. I dozed off for a few minutes. When I opened my eyes, smoke filled the room."

"Did you see anyone hanging around the premises?"

"No one." She thought back to the blackened hallway of the bed-and-breakfast and the lone lamp that had shadowed the registration desk. "The night manager left me a note with the key to the room."

The sheriff jotted something on the tablet. "Who let you in?"

"No one. The front door was open when I arrived."

"And you locked it when you went upstairs?"

"I left it the way I'd found it, Sheriff, in case someone arrived after me."

"But it was locked when I got there," Luke volunteered.

The sheriff glanced at Luke before turning his gaze back to Allison. "You sure you didn't lock the door?"

"I'm quite sure."

"I blame Cooper Wallace," Luke said as the sheriff made another notation. "It's been years since he's done any repair work on the property. Faulty wiring probably caused the fire."

The sheriff shook his head. "Now, Luke, I know you two don't see eye to eye, but he's got a lot on his plate with his campaign for the state senate."

Luke let out an exasperated breath. "He'll never get elected."

"If you came to town a bit more often, you might realize Coop's favored to win. 'Course, there's no one of worth running against him."

Wallace? The name of one of the men Allison needed to find. "Any chance he's related to Jason Wallace?"

The sheriff nodded. "Jason's his kid brother. Why?"

What could she say? She needed to respect Jason Wallace's privacy, but she also needed to answer the sheriff's question truthfully.

"I hope to talk to him later today about a test my lab is developing."

"A test that has to do with the health of the local deer population," Luke added.

The sheriff raised his brow. "Folks take their hunting seriously around these parts."

Allison glanced at the magazines on the table and the mounted deer head hanging on the wall. "So it seems."

A gust of wind whistled down the chimney, and she shivered, not so much from the cold but from the confusion she felt. The sheriff's interrogation had turned in a new direction. "Let me assure you, I didn't come to Sterling to cause trouble."

The sheriff frowned. "Some might disagree."

"Meaning?" She looked at Luke, but his eyes were veiled.

The sheriff pursed his lips. "We've never had an arson case before."

Her breath caught. "Arson?"

His gaze was direct, his tone as cold as the wind. "The fire started in the hallway outside your room, and was fueled by an accelerant."

Allison's neck tingled and a sick feeling roiled through her stomach.

"Hate to tell you, ma'am—"

She flicked another glance at Luke, who stared into the fireplace.

"From the looks of it—"

The sheriff shook his head. His voice seemed distant.

A roar filled her ears. She swallowed down the lump that clogged her throat and tried to hear what he was saying.

"From the looks of it, I'd say someone in Sterling wants you dead."

THREE

An arson case in Sterling.

Luke had a hard time swallowing that bit of information. Sure, he'd been quick to blame Cooper Wallace for neglecting the upkeep on the property, but that was a far cry from setting the fire on purpose.

Overcome with frustration, Luke kicked a pile of leaves and sent them scattering along the driveway as he waited for the sheriff to finish interrogating Allison in private. She'd insisted the details about her test remain confidential. Once he realized his presence was keeping her from explaining everything to the sheriff, Luke had excused himself and stepped outside.

Did she think he'd spread the information all over town? If only she knew how little he had to do with anyone from Sterling.

Luke turned at the sound of the door opening. Sheriff Treadwell hustled across the porch and down the steps. "Thanks for giving us a few minutes alone, Luke. Doubt her work in Atlanta has much bearing on the fire, but I'll have a talk with the three blood donors she came here to question."

"Did she tell you it might involve wasting disease?"

"Only that it was a possibility."

"I called the game warden this morning to give him a heads-up."

"Has he seen any sick game?"

"Not a one. Any idea who set the blaze?"

"Wish I did. Truth be told, I don't have a clue, but like I told Allison, because of where it started, she could be the likely target."

"Don't rule out Cooper. I'm sure he's made some enemies. Or maybe the arsonist was looking for someone who rented the room before Allison."

"Now you're thinking like a cop. I'll talk to Cooper. I've already questioned the guy he has running the B and B. From what he said, business has been slow all year. The upstairs rooms haven't been occupied for months."

"Then why'd he put Allison up there?"

"Three of the rooms on the first floor were being remodeled. He had rented the two remaining downstairs rooms earlier in the week. When Allison e-mailed for reservations, he had no choice but to put her upstairs."

"Did he tell anyone which room she was in?"

"Supposedly no one."

"Cooper would have access to that information."

The sheriff shook his head. "Now, Luke, you know Cooper's busy with his campaign. Doubtful he's interested in who's staying at the B and B or which rooms have been rented out. You're letting what happened ten years ago cloud your judgment. You gotta let it go, son. Your daddy would have been the first to tell you to forgive and forget."

The sheriff's words stung like alcohol on an open wound. "My father believed in justice. You know that, Vic."

"Best sheriff Sterling's ever had. Stepping into his shoes after his death was the hardest move I've ever made."

"Folks still giving you a hard time about never charging me with the crime?"

"Folks talk about a lot of things, you know that. First thing your dad taught me when I became a deputy was that people always talk. Can't do anything about it, so best to let it slide like water off a duck's back."

"But they haven't forgotten."

"As bad as it was, doubtful anyone will forget. But they've moved on to other things. Might do you good to follow their example. You've been holed up out here like an ostrich with your head in the sand. Time to face life again. Ten years is too long to close yourself off."

Luke stuck out his hand. "Good advice, Vic. Fact

is I'm planning to make a trip into Sterling today. There's someone I want to see."

The sheriff raised his brow. "You don't need more trouble."

"You should talk to Cooper Wallace about causing trouble."

"You're a friend, Luke. But that wasn't the reason I didn't arrest you. You know there wasn't enough evidence. Despite our friendship, and no matter how cold that case might be, if something concrete shows up that ties you to the crime, I'll haul you in faster than a hawk sweeping down on its prey. You understand me, son?"

The front door opened, and Luke turned to see Allison standing on the porch, her eyes wide, brow furrowed with question.

The sheriff tipped his head. "Ma'am, I'll keep you posted on what I find out."

He slapped Luke's shoulder, then turned and headed to his squad car.

From the confusion Luke saw written plainly on Allison's face, he wondered if she'd heard the sheriff's comment. She didn't need anything else to carry on her slender shoulders.

Talk of arson and a cold-case crime was enough to send her scurrying back to Atlanta, where, he had to admit, she'd probably be safer. After everything that had happened, Sterling was anything but safe.

* * *

Why was Luke staring at her with such a strange expression on his face? Evidently she'd interrupted a personal conversation he'd been having with the sheriff.

She would have stayed in the house, but Bett and Shelly had gone out the back door to the garden, and Allison had needed to grab her cell from the cabin and call the lab before she headed to town. Although with the medication still in her system, she wondered if she should drive. The muscle relaxers had taken the edge off the pain, but they made her feel like she was moving in slow motion. Add to the mix that she was still struggling to understand everything that had happened last night. If what Sheriff Treadwell said was true, someone had tried to kill her. Surely he was mistaken. She didn't know anyone in Sterling who would want to do her harm.

Squaring her shoulders, Allison walked down the steps to where Luke stood. "Bett said you could give me directions back to town."

Luke nodded. "I can do better than that. I'll drive you there."

He certainly aimed to please. "Don't you have work to do?"

A lazy smile pulled at the corners of his mouth. "Yes, ma'am, but it can wait."

Okay. She'd accept his offer. "Give me ten minutes to make a phone call."

Allison picked her way along the path to the cabin, feeling Luke's eyes following her. Opening the door, she glanced over her shoulder, expecting to see him still standing in the driveway, but he'd disappeared from sight.

A feeling settled over her. Relief or disappointment? She wasn't sure.

Closing the door behind her, Allison found her cell and punched in the number to the lab.

"Magnolia Medical, research department." Denise Ryan, the lab secretary, answered on the third ring. Once she heard Allison's voice, she sighed deeply.

"I was worried. The morning news mentioned a fire. Sounded like the place where you were staying."

"I'm fine, Denise. A very nice woman and her nephew took me in."

"Oh-h?" She exaggerated the word into two syllables. "And just how old is this nephew?"

Allison couldn't help but laugh. Denise loved to play matchmaker, and she'd offered Allison more than a few names of eligible bachelors. None of whom Allison had been interested in meeting. "My guess, early thirties."

"And you turned twenty-nine on your last birthday. Sounds perfect."

"Enough of that. I need to talk to Veronica."

The secretary lowered her voice. "I think she's gotten some flack about those units you quarantined yesterday, especially with the shortage we're having statewide."

Denise had reached out to Allison when she'd first received funding for her research. Always one to know the latest scuttlebutt, the secretary had quickly clued her in to Veronica's insistence on perfection. Something Allison couldn't fault.

Laboratory testing required precision and accuracy. When someone's life hung in the balance, there was no time for second-guessing. That was exactly why Allison was in Sterling. She believed her results were valid.

"Have you talked to any donors yet?" the lab manager asked as soon as she got on the line.

"That's what I plan to do today. I'll let you know what I uncover."

"The board expects a detailed explanation on why those three units are being held in quarantine. Bottom line, they don't want surgeries canceled because of a lack of blood."

"And I don't want someone to come down with a fatal disease post-transfusion from a unit that may be infected."

Veronica sighed. "Of course we have to err on the side of caution. I'll type up a report and present it to the board as soon as I hear back from you. Oh, and by the way, Allison, your dad called to talk to you this morning."

"My dad? Did he say what he wanted?"

"Evidently he got wind of your research. You didn't tell me you were Dr. Philip Stewart's daughter. He's one of the leading surgeons in this part of the country. Invite me to lunch next time he's in town."

"His schedule keeps him rather busy." Allison wouldn't mention their father-daughter estrangement to Veronica.

"I hope you don't mind, but Denise forwarded his call to me. I told him you'd hit a slight blip in your test protocol that might put your research on hold."

The positive test results were not a blip. And there was no reason her father needed to be told his daughter was less than successful. He'd figured that out long ago.

Of course, she wouldn't mention that to Veronica, either.

"Call me when you have something," her supervisor continued. "There's another South Georgia blood draw in less than two weeks."

"Ten days to be exact. I'll find the reason for the results as soon as I can. Just be sure the board doesn't release those three units of blood."

Allison hung up, feeling anxiety eat at her esophagus. She had to focus on the task at hand or all the work she'd done would go up in smoke.

Not a good analogy.

FOUR

Baling hay all day in the scorching sun had to be easier than trying to make conversation with the woman sitting in the passenger seat.

Allison had talked to the sheriff about her test in Atlanta, but she wouldn't share any additional information with Luke.

"I know you're trying to protect the people you came here to question."

"I won't divulge their names, if that's what you're fishing for."

He held up his hand. "I'm not fishing for anything. Just tell me where you need to go in town."

"Sterling Real Estate," she said, acting like she was giving away a national security secret.

Four agents worked for the real estate firm. No way Luke would know which person had the unusual blood result. He'd let Allison have her privacy.

Besides, she'd already mentioned Jason Wallace when she had talked to the sheriff. As far as Luke was concerned, the other people she needed to talk to could be any of the folks who had answered the call for blood.

He shook his head ever so slightly. The day of the blood drive he'd been in Atlanta with his editor so he hadn't been able to donate.

Luke glanced at her again. Allison was an unknown. No reason to turn his life upside down for a woman he'd only just met. Okay, he'd done exactly that, climbing onto a burning building to save a damsel in distress. Sounded chivalrous, didn't it? Although he didn't feel like anyone's knight in shining armor.

Now he was chauffeuring her into Sterling, a town he usually skirted. Ever since he'd seen her standing at the window of the B and B, he'd been filled with an overwhelming urge to protect and defend.

Sounded like he was a cop.

Although right now he felt more like a guy who couldn't put all the pieces together.

The drive to Sterling took less than twenty minutes, but in that time Luke found Allison didn't like to talk about herself or her family.

Once they neared town, he could feel his own protective defenses slipping into place. Eyes on the road, he refused to acknowledge any of the locals they passed along the way.

He'd drop Allison at Sterling Real Estate and wait for her out front. After everything that had happened last night, he didn't want her wandering around town alone.

The sheriff had mentioned arson. Had an acquaintance from Atlanta, who wanted to do her harm, followed Allison to Sterling? Or had someone in town taken offense to her questions about a disease that may involve the local deer population? Neither case boded well for Allison. She'd had one close call. Next time she might not be as lucky.

From what Allison could see, Sterling, Georgia, appeared to be a sleepy little Southern town with a central grassy square complete with a bandstand gazebo and park benches shaded by live oaks draped with Spanish moss.

Two blocks south of the square, Luke pulled into a parking space, rounded the car and held the door open for her.

"Your destination, madam." He pointed to a modest one-story brick building, where a hand-painted sign swung in the breeze. Sterling Real Estate. Established in 1954.

Allison grabbed her briefcase and purse. "Thanks, Luke. I'll call you when the interview's over."

He crossed his arms over his chest and leaned back against the car as if he didn't have a care in the world. "I'll wait for you here. Holler if you run into a problem."

Although grateful for his support, she hated to take up so much of his time.

"I'll be fine," she insisted. To prove the point, she hitched her purse over her shoulder and walked purposefully toward the door of the real estate office, wishing she felt as sure of the statement as her voice sounded. She was a medical technologist who worked in research. Tracking down outbreaks of emerging infectious diseases was not her area of expertise.

A chill settled over her as she stepped into the cool interior of the building, realizing too late she should have worn a jacket.

A secretary sat at a desk behind the counter and flipped through a stack of For Sale flyers. Allison waited patiently until the woman raised her eyes.

After giving her name, Allison said, "I have an appointment with Craig Taylor."

As the woman checked the appointment schedule, Allison glanced out the large front window to where Luke lounged lazily against the car. He winked back at her, making her smile despite the butterflies that flittered through her stomach.

"The mayor's with Craig." The secretary pointed to a closed door in the far corner of the room. "But I've got a notation for you to go in as soon as you arrive."

"Mayor?"

"Craig's dad. He owns Sterling Drug. Only pharmacist in town until he was elected mayor eight years ago." She motioned Allison forward. "Go on now. They're waiting for you."

Allison tapped on the door before she pushed it open. Two men stood behind an oak desk. The elder appeared to be in his midfifties with black hair streaked with silver. His round, pudgy face and quick smile instantly put Allison at ease.

Stepping forward, he extended his hand. "So nice to meet you, Allison. I'm Monroe Taylor, Craig's father."

He pointed to a thin man with a bottlebrush of hair that covered the tip of his pointed chin. "You talked to my son yesterday."

Craig's dull stare and nonexistent smile made her wonder how he held down a job in sales. She extended her arm to meet his limp handshake. "Thanks for agreeing to talk to me."

He motioned her toward a seat and lowered himself into the swivel chair behind his desk before she was seated. The mayor pulled a stool from the corner and placed it next to the desk, where his glance flicked from Craig to Allison.

"Craig mentioned a test you conducted on the blood he donated?"

"Yes, sir, that's correct." She smiled at both men, hoping to ease the tension in the room. Or perhaps she was the only one feeling the pressure.

"I'm working on a test that will increase the safety of our blood supply. Magnolia Medical's blood-processing center does the routine testing on each donor unit, and I've been running random samples through a procedure that's in the developmental stage. Your blood, Craig, and samples from two other people who live in Sterling reacted differently from the other specimens."

Monroe's brow wrinkled. "What does that mean? Is Craig sick?"

"I feel fine." Craig scratched his chin.

Allison held up her hand. "Let me assure both of you that at this stage the test does not indicate illness. Should something change in the future, our medical director would contact you."

Craig straightened in his chair. "Nobody asked if I wanted my blood tested."

"Authorization is not required to ensure the safety of blood for transfusion," she said.

"They routinely screen blood for hepatitis or HIV," the father explained before glancing at Allison. "Are you researching a bacterial or viral disease?"

"Actually it involves prions."

Monroe paused for a minute and then shook his head. "I've got a pharmacy degree, but I don't recall hearing that term. Of course, I attended college in the seventies. There've been a lot of changes since then."

"I don't have AIDS, do I?" Craig asked.

"My test has nothing to do with the diseases your father mentioned. Now, if you don't mind, I'd like to ask you a few questions."

Veronica had been right. Discussing the test could open a Pandora's box if Allison wasn't careful. At least she'd soothed the Taylors' concerns for the moment.

Over the next few minutes, Allison ran through a series of questions, looking for anything that might lead to the source of infection, and jotted down the responses in her notebook.

"Have you ever traveled outside the United States, perhaps to Europe or Canada?" she asked.

"Farthest I've gone is the Florida coast on vacation."

The mayor nodded in agreement.

"What about your contact with wild game? Are you a hunter, Craig?"

He shook his head.

"I never allowed guns in the house when my son was growing up," Monroe was quick to add.

"Do you eat venison and, if so, how often?"

"Craig's a vegetarian."

Allison smiled thinly at the mayor and shifted in her chair to face the son, hoping to encourage him to answer.

"How long has it been since you last ate meat?" she continued.

"About ten years," the father once again interjected.

Nodding in agreement, Craig continued to pick at his goatee, a habit that was beginning to bother

Allison. Or maybe it was the fact that the senior member of the family was far more vocal than his son.

Truth was she was back to square one. If Craig had been a vegetarian for years and didn't hunt, she'd have a hard time making a connection with wasting disease.

The first interview hadn't gone as she'd hoped, but her procedure wasn't flawed. She'd know more after she talked with the two other donors who'd tested positive.

Strike one.

Luke leaned against his SUV and watched the door to the real estate office, waiting for Allison to reappear.

Through the window, he'd seen her walk into the corner office. Craig Taylor's name hung on the door. Allison had mentioned Jason Wallace to the sheriff. Craig must be the second man with the questionable blood specimen.

Questionable described Craig. He'd been a weird kid who'd grown into an even stranger adult.

A car door slammed behind him. "Well if it isn't Luke Garrison."

He recognized the voice and groaned. Cooper Wallace.

Don't make trouble. The sheriff's words rumbled through his mind.

Luke turned to face the man who had once been his friend.

"I thought you planned to boycott town forever," the lawyer drawled, his voice as slick as a snake and just as deadly. "Someone said you don't feel welcome in Sterling."

"You never change, do you, Cooper? Always egging for a fight."

The lawyer placed his hands on his chest and feigned a surprised look. "Me? You must have the wrong guy. I was always the peacemaker."

"That's a joke. Although there were times you skirted trouble by running the other way."

Luke pulled himself upright and squared his shoulders in case Cooper forgot his good manners. Luke wouldn't start a fight, but he wouldn't step away from one, either.

"I've never run away from anything," the lawyer defended himself.

"What about our friendship?"

The look on Cooper's face told Luke he'd struck the right chord. Inseparable as boys, Cooper had turned his back on Luke quicker than anyone else. Being odd man out had been hard, especially after his dad's death. Having lost so much in such a short period of time, he wasn't about to let Cooper off the hook today.

"Your negligence almost cost four people their lives last night," Luke said.

"Evidently, you haven't talked to the sheriff. Someone set that fire."

"Were you hoping to collect on the insurance money?"

Cooper fisted his hands. "I could sue you for slander."

"You let that old house rot away so that anything could spark a fire. It was a tinderbox, ready to go up in flames."

"Why you—"

"You know it's the truth. You haven't done a bit of repair in years. Then you stick a woman on the second floor, supposedly because the first floor rooms were being remodeled. Although I can't imagine you spending money on upgrades."

"The night manager takes care of assigning guests to rooms."

"And where was he? Did you tell him to leave early?"

"Isn't that the excuse you used for Hilary's death? You had taken her home early. Then supposedly you drove back to town. But no one saw you."

"Shut up, Cooper."

"Why don't you go back to that farm you own and play like nothing happened? Write your articles for that hunting magazine and talk about gun safety all you want. The fact that your father killed himself with his hunting rifle would make a good feature story."

"It was an accident."

Cooper's eyes narrowed. "You can call it that. I call it suicide."

Luke fisted his hand.

"Luke?"

He turned at the sound of Allison's voice.

A sly grin crept across Cooper's face. "Everyone's been talking about the newcomer in town. Allison Stewart, I presume. Please accept my sincere apology for what happened."

He extended his hand, which she accepted. "I'm Cooper Wallace, and you were staying at my B and B last night."

Luke counted the seconds until they broke contact. Too long in his opinion.

"Be sure to send me an itemized statement of anything destroyed in the fire. I'll submit it to my insurance company so you can be reimbursed for your loss. Medical bills as well. I understand you were injured when Luke made you jump from the second-story window."

"And saved my life." Allison smiled at Luke, who had moved protectively closer.

He didn't trust the slick lawyer and certainly not when a pretty woman was concerned.

"Where were you last night?" Luke demanded of Cooper.

"Speaking to the Rotary Club in Macon, if you must know. Jason and I drove there in the afternoon and spent the night."

"Is your brother back in town?" Allison asked.

Cooper shook his head. "He headed on to Augusta

for a couple days to organize the eastern area of the state for my Georgia senate campaign."

Allison pulled a business card from her purse. "Would you have him call me once he gets back?"

"Of course." Cooper took the card and slipped it into his breast pocket.

"Now if you'll excuse me." He nodded to Allison. "Nice meeting you, ma'am. Please don't hesitate to let me know if you need anything at all. I'm at your service."

As Cooper walked away, Luke held open the car door for Allison. "Let's head back to the farm."

"If you don't mind taking me to the Roadside Grill, I'd like to talk to Ray Sullivan. When I stopped in last night, the waitress said he'd already left for the evening."

"So he's mystery man number three."

She hesitated.

"It's okay, Allison. Ray's a nice enough guy, and you don't have to worry about me."

The look in her eyes made him realize she didn't know if she could trust him yet. Something he'd have to prove to her over the next day or two.

He prided himself on being a man of integrity. Hopefully, she'd come to believe that was true. Even if no one else did.

The Roadside Grill looked less threatening in the light of day. Or maybe it was having Luke standing beside her that eased Allison's worry. Last night, she had been an unwelcome stranger seeking information and had instantly felt the ire of the late-night patrons. The two men who had been most vocal were nowhere to be seen today, but the waitress was back on duty.

"Why Luke Garrison," she drawled, as Allison and Luke entered the Grill. "Didn't expect to see you in town."

"Morning, Marcy." Luke nodded a greeting. "We stopped by to see Ray."

"Sit down and I'll pour you a cup of coffee. Ray had an errand to run. He'll be back shortly."

Luke motioned Allison toward a corner booth. When they'd both settled into opposite benches, the waitress appeared with two mugs, which she filled from the steaming pot of coffee she carried in her other hand.

"I heard about that fire at Coop's place. Seems the whole town's talking about how you pulled someone to safety." Her gaze flicked to Allison. "You the gal he saved?"

Luke introduced Allison to Marcy Wyatt, who eyed her for a moment before asking, "Weren't you in here last night? Those two guys sitting at the counter weren't happy about what you had to say about the venison on the menu."

"Who were they, Marcy?" Luke asked.

She shrugged. "No one I knew. Said they were

passing through." The waitress sniffed and tilted her head. "Rile up people about their huntin', then a fire almost takes your life. Too much of a coincidence, if you know what I mean."

Allison hadn't expected her few comments from the previous night to make a stir. Certainly not one that would prove life-threatening.

Marcy headed for the kitchen. "Let me know if you folks want something to eat."

Allison was ready to take her first sip of coffee when the door burst open and Sheriff Treadwell rushed inside.

"Glad I saw your car out front, Luke. I just got off the phone with Bett. She tried to call you, but your cell went to voice mail. Shelly's having one of her spells."

Luke stood before the sheriff finished speaking. He threw a five-dollar bill on the table and reached for Allison's arm as she slid from the booth.

"I'll give you a police escort," the sheriff said.

They raced to the parking lot, where a man wearing a flannel shirt and jeans pulled a can of gasoline from the bed of his pickup truck.

Luke stopped short. "What's the gas for, Ray?"

He gave Luke a blank stare. "I've gotta mow the lot behind the grill. Is that a problem?"

Allison glanced at the dry winter thatch that went dormant this time of year.

"Your gas can run dry last night?" the sheriff asked.

"Fact is someone siphoned off what I had in the shed out back."

The sheriff stared at Ray for half a second, then pointed his finger. "You stay put. I'll be back to talk to you later."

Undoubtedly he was Ray Sullivan, the man Allison needed to see. But as fast as Luke was heading to the car, this wasn't the time.

Climbing into the passenger side, Allison snapped her seat belt into place. The sheriff took the lead, lights flashing and siren screaming as the two vehicles flew down the country road.

Luke's face was tight with worry and his hands gripped the steering wheel white-knuckled, evidence of the seriousness of the situation.

Allison grabbed the door handle, digging her fingers into the leather while the siren's shrill cry tugged at the closed door to her heart.

Luke reached for his cell, pushed a prompt and held the phone to his ear. "Turn off the siren, Vic, when we round the bend to the house. You know that sound carries too many memories for Shelly."

Too many memories for Allison as well.

A lone wail cut through the air, then silenced as they banked the turn just ahead. Luke's farm sat in the distance.

The tires skidded on the concrete as he pulled into the drive and braked to a stop in front of the cabin.

Bett knelt on the porch, holding Shelly. The girl's

arms thrashed the air as if fighting off an imaginary attacker. Deep guttural sounds rose from her throat, mournful keens that chilled Allison and sent goose bumps to pimple her flesh.

Bett tried to calm the child but to no avail.

Hearing the doors slam, Shelly twisted from her aunt's grasp, scurried down the steps and raced toward the car, seemingly faster than her lopsided gait could take her.

Luke held open his arms. "Everything's going to be okay, darlin'."

Shelly skirted his embrace and threw herself at Allison, who instinctively wrapped her arms around the frantic child.

Rubbing her hand over Shelly's shoulders, she soothed her with words of comfort.

"It's okay, honey. I won't let anyone hurt you."

Almost instantly, the tension began to leave the girl's troubled body.

Allison looked up to see Luke's face filled with question. Behind him, Bett wrung her hands, her face drawn and brow furrowed. The sheriff stood by his car, the flashing lights still stabbing the air.

What had happened to throw this frightened child into such a state of frenzy?

From the bits and pieces of what Allison had heard today, the Garrisons had isolated themselves from the people in town. Shelly's mother had died following childbirth. Her father had died as well.

A tragic legacy for any child to inherit.

Allison had come to Sterling to find answers to a fatal disease. She may have stumbled onto something much more distressing.

FIVE

Once Shelly had calmed down completely, Allison walked her into the house and stood by as Bett gave her medication, which soon had her sleeping on the couch.

Why had Shelly run into Allison's arms instead of to Luke or Bett? They seemed to have a loving relationship with Shelly, and their concern for her well-being appeared genuine.

As upset as everyone seemed, this wasn't the time to broach the subject. Better to give them time to let the excitement die down and everyone's frayed nerves unwind.

Allison excused herself and started back to the cabin. On the way, she spied a path that meandered through the woods. The day had turned warm, and the sun on her back eased her strained muscles. A little exercise and fresh air would do her good.

Leaving her purse on the porch swing, she headed down a path that curved through a dense patch of pines and hardwoods. Sparrows flew through the trees as Allison strolled, enjoying the chance to escape the confusion that had troubled her earlier. The path eventually led to the edge of a clearing.

A stack of charred logs indicated an old campfire. Larger stumps appeared to have offered seating to campers who had long ago used the site.

Off to one side stood a small wooden cross, similar to those placed along highways to mark where loved ones had tragically died. Once white, now only traces remained of the original paint that had soaked into the deep recesses of the weathered wood.

The distance from Luke's house was under a mile. Had someone died in this clearing? Perhaps someone in Luke's family? Eerie, really, when added to what she'd witnessed earlier. A special child haunted by horrific images had broken down in her arms. Shelly's parents died before their time. Did their deaths have something to do with this splintered cross? Or had some other life been snuffed out in these deep, dark woods.

For an instant in her mind's eye, Allison saw the campfire blaze and tongues of fire dart skyward as if demons fanned the flames seeking another person for their ritualistic sacrifice.

She shook off the thought, not willing to dwell on such a ghoulish possibility.

An unexpected gust of wind chilled Allison. She shivered and rubbed her hands over her arms for warmth.

She'd strayed too far and been gone longer than she'd planned.

Leaves rustled to her left. Allison caught movement out of the corner of her eye. A furry head rose from the underbrush.

Just a squirrel.

She turned back to the path.

Seconds later, stillness settled over the forest, causing a nervous tingle to play along her neck. She rubbed her arms again, hoping to ward off the strange sensation that filtered through her.

Unnerving, really.

Almost as if she were being watched.

"Get a grip." She laughed, hearing an edge of unease mixed with the sarcasm.

She increased her pace until pain in the small of her back caused her to stop. Once again she sensed a presence.

Slowly, she turned.

Her heart lunged in her chest.

A deer stood not more than eight feet away. From the wide spread of antlers, undoubtedly a buck, with a sleek chestnut coat that appeared healthy. No hint of disease.

But too close for comfort.

Allison took a step back, then another.

The animal glared at her with stern brown eyes.

"Nice, Bambi," she mumbled, hearing the tremble in her voice.

Its flank twitched, and without warning the buck charged.

Allison screamed and covered her face. The sound of pummeling hooves filled the air along with the whoosh of an object hurling past her.

Hands grabbed her. With a quick sidestep, Luke stood in front of her.

"He-aw-w-w!" he screamed at the buck.

Startled, the animal changed direction and galloped off into the forest.

Allison gasped with relief.

Luke let out a deep breath and turned to face her, his hand protectively on her waist. "Are you okay?"

She nodded, trying to find her voice. "I…I didn't expect the deer to charge."

"He's in rut. Bucks get aggressive and territorial this time of year. He could have killed you."

"Seems you've saved my life once again." She attempted to smile despite hot tears that stung her eyes.

Grappling with the swell of emotions that churned within her, she turned her head and spied a huge hunting knife stuck in the trunk of a mighty oak.

Luke followed her gaze.

"Looks like you missed," she said, feeling a sense of confusion sweep over her.

"I wasn't trying to hit the deer, just spook him." His hand dropped from her waist, and he stepped toward the tree.

She hadn't noticed him wearing a knife earlier. "Do you always carry a weapon when you walk in the woods?"

He glanced back at her and raised his brow. "As you found out, some of God's creatures aren't friendly."

"A shotgun might offer better protection."

He shimmied the knife from the tree. The silver blade gleamed as he wiped it along his pants, then shoved it into the leather sheath that hung from his belt. "The knife serves the purpose."

She crossed her arms over her chest. "Did you grab the weapon when you decided to follow me?"

"I didn't *decide* to follow you. I glanced out the window and saw you heading into the woods. Things happen, as you just found out. Plus, you seem to attract trouble."

Trouble? She huffed and turned on her heel.

Then she caught sight of the cross through the trees and shuddered, thinking again of everyone who had died. Life or death? It seemed, at least in this area of the world, that death had the upper hand.

"Bett will be worried," she said over her shoulder as she hurried along the path that led to the cabin.

Bett wasn't the only one who might worry. At this point, Allison was worried as well. What was really happening in Sterling?

* * *

Luke watched Allison charge ahead.

Why had she chosen this particular path that led to the clearing?

He was surprised she'd even decided to take a stroll, what with her aching back. If she had wanted to walk, she could have stayed on the road that fronted the house. Somehow the city girl didn't seem like she belonged in the dense forest.

His gut tightened as he glanced back at the wooden cross. As much as he wanted to bury the past, everything seemed to be bubbling to the surface once again.

With a frustrated sigh, he hastened to catch up with Allison. One thing was for sure—their tranquil life had been disrupted since her arrival.

His sister hadn't had a severe episode in over eight months. Yet today she'd had a major meltdown. What surprised him most was that she'd run to Allison for comfort, a person she'd only just met.

Bett said Shelly's attack had started when she'd gone to the cabin and found it empty. The doctors claimed his mentally and physically challenged sister's perception of reality would always be skewed. In her mixed-up mind, had she confused Allison with Hilary?

Luke shook his head ever so slightly. What was he supposed to do? The Lord knew he'd tried to fill the gaps in Shelly's life. Recently, he'd thought he'd seen improvement. Of course, the doctors hadn't agreed.

Her episode today proved they were right.

As the path broke from the forest, Allison scurried toward the cabin, where her purse sat on the swing. A repetitive trill signaled an incoming call on her cell.

She checked the caller identification before pulling the phone to her ear. "Yes, Veronica."

Allison listened for a moment then asked, "Did they change the date?"

Luke didn't want to eavesdrop, but the worry that washed across her face told him the news on the other end of the line must not be good.

Her brow furrowed. "I don't know if I'll have answers by then." She paused. "You've got to convince them I need more time."

Allison flipped her phone closed and turned to Luke. "They've moved up the date of the next blood draw in this area due to the statewide shortage."

"I know you're worried about the safety of the blood supply, but I called the game warden this morning. Georgia instituted a deer surveillance program in 2002, and they have yet to detect any animals with wasting disease. You saw that buck today. He was healthy."

"That's one animal, Luke. Besides, you don't understand."

No, he didn't understand because she refused to share anything with him except that she'd had some unexpected results on a test she was developing for her lab. A test that had to do with wasting disease in deer and with donated blood units.

From the one-sided conversation he'd just overheard, it seemed the person on the other end of the line was on her side, but what about the decision-makers who had moved up the date for the next blood draw? Evidently they didn't buy into Allison's theory.

Was she deluding herself by turning a faulty test procedure into something it wasn't? From where he stood, it seemed she might be making a lot of hoopla over nothing.

As dusk fell, the rich smell of that night's supper wafted through the open window in the cabin, tempting Allison to venture toward the main house.

Bett stepped onto the porch and waved her inside. "I was fixin' to send Luke over to get you. Roasted chicken, mashed potatoes, green beans from the garden and fresh peach pie."

Allison thought of her usual fare of frozen entrées and almost laughed. "A girl could get used to this country life."

The older woman's eyes twinkled, looking surprisingly like Shelly's when she had scrunched up her face at the sheriff's "Sunshine" comment.

Allison followed Bett into the house, where light from the lamps brightened the corners of the expansive great room. The same room that had seemed cold that morning now appeared inviting. Even the mounted deer head over the mantel took on a gentle air compared to the creature Allison had faced in the woods.

Glancing into a lit alcove she hadn't noticed earlier, Allison spied a glass case hanging above a rolltop desk. Displayed within the case was a knife similar to the one Luke had brandished earlier.

Bett followed her gaze. "The original Garrison hunting knife. Belonged to our great-grandfather. He forged the steel blade, carved the handle."

Pride was evident in Bett's voice as she continued. "Became a tradition in the family that every male do the same. Sort of a coming-of-age rite of passage. Not long ago, Luke started a manufacturing company to reproduce replicas of our great-granddad's original work."

"And he wears the knife when he's in the woods?" Allison asked.

"Always."

Bett's simple explanation of the significance of the hunting knife eased Allison's concerns about what had happened earlier.

The older woman touched Allison's arm and motioned her forward. "Supper's getting cold."

"How's Shelly?" Allison asked as they made their way toward the kitchen.

"She slept for much of the afternoon. When she woke, she seemed her old self. She'll probably be up most of the night, but at least her anxiety has calmed. Breaks my heart to see her like that. What's a mo—"

She turned and smiled sheepishly. "I almost said mother. Fact is, the child seems like my own."

"If you don't mind my asking, what happened to Mrs. Garrison?"

Bett stopped her forward progression and turned sorrow-laden eyes toward Allison.

"You hear more about it these days, but when Shelly was born, most folks around here didn't talk about postpartum depression. Shelly was a late-in-life baby, and her birth was difficult for Miriam. For a number of hours, the midwife didn't know if mom or baby would survive."

Bett shook her head slowly as if the memory weighed heavy on her heart. "I don't know if it was the long labor and traumatic delivery or Miriam's being worn-out and without the energy to fight back, but it seemed she just gave up."

A sense of loss swept over Allison.

"Luke was serving in the army at the time. Luckily, I'd moved back home and was living in the cabin, debating what to do with my life. After Miriam died, there wasn't any doubt that I'd stay."

"And you've been here ever since?"

"That's right. Can't complain, though. I have a beautiful child to care for and a purpose for living. The Good Lord knew where I needed to be. Luckily, I listened to His call."

Bett started toward the kitchen and then hesitated, raising her eyes once again to meet Allison's.

"What about you, dear? Do you have a family?"

Allison thought of her father, who had closed her out of his life, and her mother, who wouldn't counter what her husband said. She and Allison met each month for lunch in Atlanta, but since Allison had left for college after the accident, she had never gone back home.

"I don't have time for family." A lie, but it was the best she could offer.

"What about the Lord? Do you have time for Him?"

She didn't know how to answer Bett. Making time for the Lord had never been a priority. He hadn't listened to her prayers for help when she'd begged Him to let Drew live. Why would He be interested in anything she had to say now?

"God doesn't seem tuned in to my wavelength."

"Sometimes we're the ones who aren't tuned in," Bett said, her gaze knowing. She patted Allison's arm reassuringly, then turned and pushed open the swinging door to the kitchen.

Shelly's guttural sounds mixed with Luke's laughter and spilled into the hallway, where Allison stood, not knowing if she was ready to move forward.

Luke lifted his eyes from the book he was reading to Shelly. His smile was warm and inviting.

The Garrisons had problems, seemingly big problems, yet they hadn't given up on the Lord.

Shelly's lips twitched into a hint of a smile of welcome.

Allison didn't know what would happen tomorrow. But just for tonight, she wanted to forget about disease and death and the cross in the woods.

She wanted to be part of a family where people loved one another and focused on their potential for success instead of their failure. Just so her need for acceptance wouldn't compromise her safety in the days ahead.

If only her time in Sterling would lead to answers she desperately needed.

She looked into Luke's eyes. Perhaps her visit would lead to other questions she would have to answer as well.

SIX

That night, Allison left the window open a crack, enjoying the cool breeze that brought the fresh scent of the outdoors into the cabin.

The clock struck midnight, yet she couldn't sleep. Probably the excitement of the day, which seemed to swirl through her mind. Or perhaps it was the brimming plate Bett had placed before her at supper. Not wanting to seem impolite, she'd eaten most of her food, enjoying the Southern home cooking and the companionship of family, which she'd missed for so long.

If she weren't allowed to continue her research, what would she tell her father? That she'd failed again?

She envisioned the knowing glint in his eye, the tilt of his head and the slight nod that said more about his reaction than any words he could utter.

He had never expected her to succeed. She was the impetuous child, the one who raced headlong into life without measuring the consequences. Her vision was flawed, he'd been quick to mention on more than one occasion. Carry the scenario out full term, he cautioned, to determine if the risk was worth the effort.

Risk and failure.

A repetitive pattern in her life.

Seemed she hadn't learned her lesson yet.

Allison grabbed the hooded velour sweatshirt that matched the baggy pants she had changed into earlier and slipped it over her T-shirt.

Padding to the small kitchen area, she brewed a cup of herbal tea and, mug in hand, headed back to the couch, hoping to soothe her jangled nerves into sleep mode.

She glanced out the window, catching sight of Luke's dark house. The Garrisons were probably sound asleep. Just as she should be.

Allison took a sip of tea, then rested her head against the back of the couch, her eyes heavy.

At that instant, gunshots rang in the distance.

She bolted upright, spilling the hot tea over her leg. Brushing a napkin over the spilled liquid, she placed her cup on the coffee table and stood, just as the cabin fell into darkness.

The tick-tock of the electric wall clock stilled, along with the hum of the refrigerator.

What could have caused the power failure?

The darkness crept around Allison, palpable as a living being. Her heart rose in her throat and fear wrapped its ugly arm around her.

Luke jerked awake as the gunshots sounded in the night. Poachers illegally hunting after dark.

He had fallen asleep on the couch, watching embers in the fireplace that had died hours ago. Now fully awake, he glanced out the window to the cabin. From the lights in the windows, Allison must be up. Working late or had she been awakened by the gunshots as well?

He should check on Shelly. The way the temperature was dropping she might be cold. He'd pull a quilt from the closet and cover her before she woke with a chill.

Mounting the stairs, he slipped into her room.

His heart lunged against his chest. Her bed was empty, the bedding rumpled, the covers thrown onto the floor.

The memory of that night so long ago returned unbidden. But he didn't have time to dwell on the past. He had to find Shelly.

Racing through the house, Luke checked each nook and cranny where Shelly might be hiding, all for naught. He wouldn't wake Bett. She had enough to worry about.

Maybe Shelly had stumbled outside into the night in hopes of seeing Allison.

Luke flew down the stairs and stepped onto the porch. The cabin was dark.

Had Allison gone to bed?

He grabbed a flashlight and raced forward, needing to see if Shelly was there. Maybe needing Allison's calm reassurance as well.

A tap-tap-tap cut through the stillness.

"Who is it?" Allison called out from the darkened room which was lit only with candles she'd found in the kitchen.

Recognizing the low moan, she opened the door.

Not waiting for an invitation, Shelly burst into the room and wrapped her arms tightly around Allison.

"Are you okay?"

Twisting out of Allison's hold, the girl shuffled into the living area and plopped down on the over-stuffed couch.

"The electricity is off, but I'm sure it will come on soon." Allison lit another candle and welcomed the light that now filled the cabin. "Do Luke and Bett know you're here?"

Shelly tilted her head, looking somewhat confused.

"They'll be worried about you." Allison took Shelly's hand and tried to pull her up, but she wedged herself farther back against the cushions.

Bett had said the child had slept most of the afternoon. Now she seemed wide-awake. After her outbreak earlier, Allison didn't want to upset her further, yet she knew her brother and aunt would be worried if they discovered Shelly's empty bed.

Better to walk Shelly home than startle Luke and Bett with a phone call at this time of night.

Before Allison could usher her to the door, Shelly charged for the fireplace, one leg dragging behind her, and patted her hand along the stacked stones as if searching for something.

"Careful," Allison warned, fearing the jagged edges might scrape Shelly's flesh. "What is it, honey? What are you looking for?"

While Shelly's eyes focused on the fireplace, questioning sounds escaped her lips that gave Allison no clue as to what she was trying to locate.

Before Allison could grab her hand, Shelly pulled one of the wedged stones free, then stuck her fingers into the gaping hole. She removed a photo from the hiding spot and held it up proudly for Allison to see.

A woman, probably in her late twenties, with raven hair and a wide smile, stood with her arms around a much younger Shelly in front of the cabin.

"Who's the lady with you?" Knowing Shelly would never answer, Allison turned the photo over. Someone had written two names: Hilary and Shelly.

Shelly took the photo and put it against her heart.

"Hilary must have been a good friend."

Shoving her hand back into the hole, Shelly

pulled out a second photo, this one somewhat faded. After smoothing the edges, she held it up to Allison.

Bett and another woman stood on the drive in front of the main house. The woman looked like Luke with her square jaw, thick chestnut hair and wide, dark eyes.

Bett's features mirrored Shelly's then as they did today.

The other woman, who favored Luke, was large with child. What startled Allison most was that Bett's stomach had the same round swell of pregnancy.

Surprise washed over Shelly's face as footsteps sounded on the porch. She shoved the faded photo back into the secret cubbyhole. Allison's stomach tightened as the footfalls stopped just outside the door. She wrapped her arms protectively around Shelly.

"Allison, it's Luke. Have you—?"

Before he could complete the question, she raced to the door and threw it open. "Shelly's in here."

Relief swept over his face. "I was so worried." He moved quickly to where his sister stood by the fireplace. Wrapping her in his arms, he turned questioning eyes to Allison.

"She hasn't been here long," she explained. "Just since the electricity went off."

Luke needed to check the circuit breakers to see what the problem was, but he put his fingers under Shelly's chin and turned her face up. "You know you're not supposed to go outside without telling Bett or me."

Shelly stole a furtive glance at Allison before she raised the photo she still held for Luke to see.

He let out a long sigh. "I know you miss Hilary. We all do."

Once again, he pulled Shelly close and kissed the top of her head.

Allison wished she could be someplace else. The tender brother-sister connection seemed too private for someone who had just dropped into these people's lives. They had a history that involved the woman in the photo.

From the look on Luke's face, evidently God hadn't answered all their prayers. Just like He hadn't answered Allison's. Yet Luke and Bett still considered Him a loving Lord.

Hope. Was that what she needed?

Maybe then she'd believe that her relationship with her father would improve. Or that she'd find the answers to the results that undermined her ability to continue her research. Or that life could be more than work and struggle and ugly consequences that weighed heavy on her heart.

Some things were too hard to accept. Like faith in God. Love. Family. She'd left them behind. They had no place in her life now or ever.

She needed facts that could be explained in a

logical way. Not some pie-in-the-sky talk about a loving God and the power of prayer.

Then she looked at the love in Luke's eyes as he held his baby sister, and she realized the very things she said she didn't want were what she needed the most.

Still clutching the photo, Shelly pulled out of Luke's arms and scooted to the couch. She snuggled into the corner cushions and stared at the picture of Hilary.

He glanced at Allison and smiled sheepishly. "I imagined all sorts of things."

"Of course you did." She headed to the kitchen. "Cup of tea sound okay?"

He was more of a coffee drinker, but he appreciated the offer. "Sounds good. I'll have the lights on in a flash."

He tripped the circuit breakers, but the cabin remained dark and the power off.

"The main disconnect is on the side of the building," he called to Allison as he stepped outside and hustled to the far end of the cabin.

Luke aimed his flashlight at the metal box and pulled off the cover. What he saw made his pulse pick up a notch.

The breaker was in the disconnect position.

A nervous rumble roiled through his gut. Who or what had thrown the switch?

Staring into the darkness, he searched for some sign of another presence, but saw nothing.

Finally, convinced the person had long gone, Luke flipped the breaker and the cabin filled with light.

He found Allison in the kitchen. "It was a glitch with the outside disconnect." He didn't share his own concerns that someone had purposefully thrown the switch.

"Thanks for fixing the problem," she said with a smile.

Luke tried to shake off the nervous edge that had settled over him ever since he'd found Shelly's empty bed. The power failure compounded his unease. Could the poachers have been up to no good? He had notified the game warden other nights when he'd heard their gunfire. Were they getting back at him tonight?

He looked at Allison busying herself in the kitchen. Could it somehow tie in with the fire at the B and B and someone's attempt to harm Allison?

She handed him a filled mug.

"Thanks." This wasn't the time or place to discuss what could have happened. Allison didn't need anything else to cause her worry. He'd enjoy the tea she offered and a chance to get to know her better before he headed back to the house and settled Shelly into bed.

Then he'd take up residence on the front porch. He'd watch the cabin through the night to ensure nothing else happened.

Oblivious to the possible threat that could be hovering outside, Allison poured milk into a glass and filled a plate with cookies she found in the cupboard, then placed them on the coffee table in front of Shelly.

"Hilary must have been a special lady," Allison said, returning to the kitchen area.

"She and Shelly bonded almost immediately." He glanced at his sister contentedly eating a cookie and smiled. "Although I think you have her beat. The doctors said she perceives things differently, but she has a good sense of who to trust. You won her over with your warmth and genuineness."

Allison wrinkled her brow.

"What? You don't see yourself that way?" he asked.

"I didn't expect the comment, that's all." She busied herself at the stove. "Folks I know rarely talk about human attributes."

"What about your family?"

"My father used to say I lacked foresight. I doubt he'd agree with your assessment."

"He's still alive?"

She smiled ruefully. "Dr. Philip Stewart, a leading surgeon in the southeast."

"You followed in his footsteps."

She lowered her gaze and wiped her hand over the counter. "My twin brother was the one who wanted to be a doctor."

"Wanted to? What changed his plans?"

"A careless drive by two stupid teens on a rainy night when both of them should have been home in bed."

"You and your brother?"

"Part of the string of bad choices I've been prone to make, or so my father likes to remind me."

"So you blame yourself."

"I'm the one who lived, Luke."

"And that puts the burden of guilt on you, in your father's opinion."

She pointed her finger at him in gun fashion. "Bingo!"

"And because he blames you, you blame yourself."

She shrugged and leaned against the counter, arms folded over her chest. When she looked at him again, her eyes were distant.

"My friends were going to a party at a guy's house who lived a few miles away. I was seventeen. It was just a couple weeks before high school graduation. You know how teenagers are. Life revolves around them. I liked the guy, but he was older, and my father thought he was too wild for his daughter. So I snuck out and caught a ride with one of my girlfriends."

"Your brother didn't go?"

"Andrew?" She looked out the window into the night. "Drew, as most folks called him, was studying for exams, but he said he'd pick me up later."

"And you had the accident on the way home?"

"There was a hairpin curve. The car was going faster than either of us realized. The high beams of an approaching car momentarily blinded us. We skidded off the road. Crashed into a giant oak. Crashed and burned, as the saying goes."

"I'm sorry, Allison."

She reached for her mug on the counter. "And I'm sorry I gave you more information than you needed or wanted. We were talking about fathers. I'm sure you miss your dad."

Luke nodded. "He was a great guy. Bigger than life, if you know what I mean. He seemed to know the answers to any question I posed. And he was always right."

"Your dad was a farmer?"

"Of sorts. His main passion was justice and the rule of law, but he and Bett were orphaned young so he never went to college. When the county needed a sheriff, some men from town asked my dad to run. They recognized his ability to ferret out the truth. He was good at what he did."

"You said his death was an accident?"

"While he was cleaning his gun. He took out the magazine, but he must have forgotten there was a bullet left in the chamber. I found him in the barn by the south pasture where he stored his weapons. Shelly was little, and he didn't want guns in the house."

He glanced at his sister, whose eyes had closed.

"Bett and I were so worried about Shelly that we hardly had time to grieve. She had been hospitalized a couple weeks earlier. After Dad's death, Bett and I took turns staying with her round the clock. The doctors weren't optimistic."

"Because of your father's accident?"

"That fell on the heels of another tragedy."

She raised her brow, waiting for him to go on, but the silence grew between them.

"Evidently it's something you don't want to talk about," she finally said, taking a sip from her cup of tea.

Allison had confided in him about her brother's death, but Luke wasn't ready to share every detail of his past. She'd be heading back to Atlanta in a day or two. No reason to tell all to a short-term friend who would soon be moving on.

"If you want to talk to Ray tomorrow, I'll drive you back to town," he finally said.

"I thought you stayed clear of Sterling?"

"Most folks believe my father committed suicide. I don't want Shelly to hear their idle chatter."

"You can't protect her forever, Luke."

"Probably not, but I can try. Other than Bett, I'm all the family she has. It falls on my shoulders to take care of her. People can be cruel. I know they make fun of her handicap." He shook his head. "I can't stand to see her hurt."

"She's a sweet girl. Maybe if they get to know her, they'll change their attitude."

"It's a chance I don't want to take." He placed the mug on the counter. "I better say good-night and take Shelly back to the house before Bett wakes and finds us both missing."

He lifted his still-sleeping sister into his arms and carried her to the door, which Allison held open.

"We'll head to town after breakfast," Luke said before he stepped outside.

The sooner Allison talked to Ray Sullivan and Jason Wallace, the sooner she'd head back to Atlanta. Luke needed to protect Shelly from the outside world, and that included Allison.

He'd be glad when she left. Then he looked over his shoulder and saw her standing at the door.

Or would he?

After breakfast, Allison slipped into the passenger seat of Luke's SUV.

Inside the house, she hadn't noticed the lines around his eyes or his drawn face. "You look tired."

He glanced at the rocker on the front porch and shrugged. "Restless night, that's all."

Allison could relate. She hadn't slept well, either.

When they entered the Roadside Grill, a number

of tables still needed to be bussed, confirming business was good. No wonder Ray was smiling as he rang up a customer and counted out the man's change. His facial expression changed when he spotted Luke and Allison.

Luke put his hand on the small of Allison's back and ushered her toward a booth, where Marcy soon attended to them and poured them coffee.

Ray approached when the last customer left the diner.

Pots and pans clanged in the kitchen. Ray caught Marcy's eye. "Why don't you take your break now."

She wiped her hands on a dishrag and grabbed her purse. "I'll be out back."

When the rear door closed behind her, Ray drew up a straight chair, straddled it and let out a deep breath. "What's going on? The sheriff talked to me yesterday and mentioned a blood test."

Allison looked at Luke. "Maybe you should join Marcy outside?"

Once they were alone, Ray leaned in closer. "It doesn't involve a sexually transmitted disease, does it?"

Ray and Craig thought alike.

She quickly reassured Ray, pulled her notebook from her purse and prefaced her questions with the same general comments she had given the mayor and his son. The test was in the developmental stage. She merely needed information.

"Have you ever traveled outside the United States?"

Ray shook his head. "The Grill keeps me close to home. Don't think I've taken a vacation in six or seven years. Business is good so I can't complain."

"Do you serve beef or any commercially prepared product that may contain beef gelatin or extract from outside this country?"

"No."

Allison didn't know whether to be relieved or frustrated.

"Do you hunt?"

"Used to. Like I said, running a restaurant is a full-time job." He scratched his cheek. "Last time must have been about six years ago. Came home with a five-point buck." He pointed to the large deer head over the corner fireplace.

"Did the animal appear diseased or disoriented?"

Ray shook his head. "Best specimen I've ever shot. The buck was fit."

Allison noted Ray's answer in her notebook.

"And you dressed the buck and ate the venison?"

"That's right."

"Where do you get the venison you serve in your restaurant?"

"A lawyer named Wallace introduced me to a hunter who runs a processing plant over in the next county."

"Cooper Wallace?"

"That's right. His friend's the major distributor I use, but I've bought from meat lockers and processing plants all over South Georgia."

Could Cooper's friend be the link between his brother and Ray? But what about Craig, who claimed to be a vegetarian?

She glanced through the window to where Luke waited on the porch.

Best sausage you'll ever eat. Bett's words played through Allison's mind. Could Bett be infected?

Or Shelly?

"You're saying there's nothing I need to worry about?" Ray asked when Allison ran out of questions.

"Developing a new test is a lengthy and costly procedure, Ray. It's too early to say more than there seems to be a connection between three people in Sterling."

Voices sounded on the porch and she looked up just as the door opened. Cooper Wallace bounded inside.

Luke stuck his head through the door and glanced from Cooper to Ray and back to Cooper. "I'm out front if you need me, Allison."

She smiled, appreciating his concern. "Thanks."

"Grab a place to sit, Coop, and I'll bring you a menu and a cup of coffee."

The lawyer held up his hand. "Stay where you are, Ray. I saw Luke sniffing around and hoped I'd find Allison inside."

"Have you heard from your brother?" she asked.

"He'll be back in Sterling tomorrow. You can talk to him then."

Ray scooted his chair back and rubbed his chin. "You mentioned three people in Sterling came up positive on that test of yours. So Jason was one of them?"

Cooper nodded. "The mayor said she was quizzing Craig yesterday."

So much for maintaining privacy.

Ray's brow wrinkled. "The only connection that comes to mind is Sterling Manor."

Allison looked up. "What?"

"A school for boys who had—" Cooper paused as he eyed Ray. "The boys had gotten in trouble for one thing or another growing up. Nothing serious, mind you."

"You mean a school for boys with behavior problems?"

"It closed the fall of our senior year," Ray chimed in. "We all transferred to the county high."

"Sits a couple miles from Luke's place," Cooper added. "Just past the second fork in the road."

"Why'd the school close?" she asked.

Cooper pursed his lips. "Luke didn't tell you?"

"'Cause of that woman who'd rented the Garrisons' cabin," Ray quickly volunteered.

"Hilary?"

"That's right. The school closed right after she was murdered."

Allison's chest tightened.

"They found her body halfway between Luke's house and the school," Ray continued.

The room swirled around Allison.

"Hilary worked as a nanny for Professor Hightower. He ran the school and took it hard. Closed the Manor right after her death."

Ray sniffed. "Most folks thought Luke Garrison had killed her. They'd been seen together earlier that night. He claimed she'd been having another one of those bad headaches she complained about. Funny that he was the one who found her body. Said he was looking for that crazy sister of his. She must have seen what happened 'cause she had some kind of a breakdown and stopped talking."

Throat dry, pulse racing, Allison closed her eyes and dug her fingernails into the booth's Naugahyde seat cushion.

"His dad was the sheriff," Ray rambled on. "Two weeks later he shot himself. Most folks think he couldn't live with the fact his son was a murderer."

Allison tried to breathe, but she couldn't pull in enough air.

Why hadn't Luke told her Hilary had been murdered? Or that he had been the last person to see her alive?

A roar filled her ears.

She grabbed her notebook and purse, her hands shaking as she stood. She needed to leave this town, with its secrets from the past, where too many people had died. People whose lives had touched Luke's.

Someone wanted you dead. The sheriff's words played through her mind. He seemed to be sweet on Bett, so she couldn't confide her concerns to him.

Where could she turn?

At this point she didn't feel safe with anyone in Sterling. She glanced outside.

Not even Luke?

SEVEN

Luke watched Allison storm out of the Grill and walk determinedly toward the SUV.

He raced after her. "What happened in there? Did Cooper hurt you? If he did, I'll—"

He turned, ready to charge back inside and teach Cooper a lesson.

"Luke!" Allison's voice was insistent. "No one did anything to me. Now, open the car door and take me back to the cabin."

The atmosphere in the SUV was chilly on the way to the farm. Allison stared straight ahead at the road. When he asked her how the interview had gone, she merely shrugged.

He could take a hint. She didn't want to talk, especially to him.

He blamed Cooper Wallace. When Coop had first entered the restaurant, Luke had checked on Allison. She'd flashed him a smile and said everything was okay.

Less than five minutes later, she had stormed outside, like the Ice Queen, ignoring his attempt at conversation.

Didn't she realize the lawyer couldn't be trusted? He cared little about his property and even less about the people he said he wanted to serve should he be elected to public office.

Frustration welled up in Luke as he tried to imagine what Cooper had told her.

He'd probably mentioned the dysfunctional Garrison family. A mother who had suffered postpartum depression after the birth of her handicapped child. A father who most folks thought had taken his own life two weeks after—

Hilary. That was it.

"Cooper told you what happened in the clearing, didn't he?"

Allison's face tightened, but she didn't say a word.

"You probably wonder why I didn't mention her death."

He must have hit the nail on the head because she finally had something to say.

"Why didn't you tell me she'd been murdered?"

"I didn't think you needed the details."

"Cooper said you had dropped her off at the cabin and had then driven to town."

Luke's hands gripped the steering wheel. He thought back to that fateful night.

"Bett was getting the flu and worried her fever might go up in the night. We didn't have any aspirin so I drove to the drugstore. But I had a flat tire on the way and got there after Monroe had closed for the night. I could see him inside the pharmacy talking to someone on the phone. Before I could get his attention, he left through the rear door. I raced around the building, but he'd already driven away."

Luke took a deep breath. "When I got back to the house, Bett was asleep. I went to check on Shelly and realized she wasn't in her room. She spent a lot of time with Hilary so I ran to the cabin." Just as he'd done last night.

Allison turned ever so slightly toward him. At least she was listening.

"I found Hilary's sweater in the woods and raced down the path to the clearing. There was blood everywhere. For a minute I didn't know whether it was Hilary's or Shelly's. I've never—"

He swallowed hard. "I've never seen such carnage."

"And Shelly?"

"She was hiding nearby, trembling uncontrollably. Her eyes were glazed over, and she couldn't focus on anything. I'm not sure she even knew who carried her back to the house. My dad was on patrol that night, but he got there in less than three minutes. When the ambulances arrived, they took Shelly to the hospital in Atlanta."

"And her breakdown yesterday tied in with Hilary's death."

Luke nodded. "She and Hilary were close. Shelly cares for you as well. I think her faulty processing skills jumbled the two of you together. Yesterday, she must have thought something had happened to you."

Allison turned toward the window. "I kept thinking about the cross in the clearing, wondering who had died there. I never suspected Hilary. No wonder Shelly wanted to find her picture that night the power went off. She wanted to show me her friend who had died." Allison shook her head, her voice thick with emotion. "I didn't come here to upset your family, Luke."

What could he say in response? Ever since Allison had fallen into their lives, the door to the past had ripped open, and Luke knew nothing would ever be the same. Half of him regretted her interference. And the other half?

He still wasn't sure how he felt.

The farm appeared in the distance. Luke turned into the drive and saw Shelly sitting on the cabin steps. She ran toward the SUV and threw her arms around Allison when she stepped from the car.

Allison kissed the top of her forehead and then gently untangled herself from Shelly's grasp.

"Come here, honey," Luke coaxed.

"I need to make some phone calls." Allison turned her back on both of them, climbed the porch steps and pushed open the cabin door. It slammed behind her, and the dead bolt dropped into place.

Shelly tried to wiggle free, but Luke held her tight against his side and ushered her toward the house.

"Allison has work to do. Let's find Bett. Maybe she'll fix us a glass of sweet tea."

Shelly's eyes remained fixed on the cabin.

Luke's heart broke for his sister. Once again, she'd become attached to someone who would disappear from her life. He should have known better than to provide lodging for a stranger.

Although after hearing about Hilary's death, he doubted Allison would stay any longer.

Not that he blamed her.

Luke wiped his feet on the doormat and stepped into the house, still holding his sister close. He hadn't been able to protect Shelly from being hurt, although he'd promised God he'd fill his father's shoes. As much as he'd tried, he'd let his dad down. As well as God.

Bett called out a greeting, and Shelly ran to join her in the kitchen.

Luke closed the door behind him and followed after his sister until the sound of a car engine caught his attention. He glanced through the window to see Allison at the wheel. She raced out of the driveway and turned toward town.

Was she going back to Sterling to find out more information from Cooper? There wasn't anything else to tell. Except that most people thought Luke had committed the crime.

That had torn his dad in two—that the town where they'd lived and worked and gone to church had turned its back on his family when they were so in need.

Now Allison had turned her back on them as well.

Good riddance, he mumbled, knowing they were only words. Reality was, he wanted her to stay.

Allison had seen the turnoff when Luke had driven her back to the house. From what Cooper had said, the road led to Sterling Manor. A school everyone had failed to mention until today.

Seems folks had failed to mention other important details as well. Like Hilary's brutal murder and Luke's possible involvement.

Allison hadn't been able to think of anything else since Ray and Cooper had filled her in on the horrific details. Yet at the same time, they'd handed her the first real clue that might solve the mystery surrounding her three positive test results.

She found the fork in the road and made the turn, wondering if she was following another wild-goose chase.

Three men in Sterling and they had all attended a special school for kids with problems. Was that the connection for which she'd been looking?

Through the trees, a large two-story antebellum

home peered out at her as if aware of her approach. Four chimneys built of bloodred brick stretched into the dismal autumn sky. Clouds blocked the sun and sent shadows to skitter over the cracked and peeling facade.

Georgia clay clogged the steps Allison climbed to the expansive portico held aloft by four massive columns. On the oak door, a brass gargoyle knocker hung like a sentinel standing guard.

She tried the knob. Locked.

A tarnished bass plaque next to the entry read, Sterling Manor. Excellence in Education.

Pressing against the window, she peered into a room filled with a carved antique desk, floor-to-ceiling bookcases and two Queen Anne chairs. A few papers lay scattered across the hardwood floor.

Surely there was a way to get inside.

Rounding the side of the house, Allison was forced to stop by a thick wall of blackberry bushes that circled the rear of the property.

She tried to push through the dense, natural barrier and cried out as the long thorns dug into her flesh, drawing blood.

Nothing serious, but seeing the dark red droplets brought a thought to mind. Had the bushes been planted to keep the curious out or the troubled boys in?

She drew a tissue from her purse and dabbed at the scratches until the bleeding stopped. Then, stretching on tiptoe, she peered over the brambles and counted three outbuildings within the protected area.

Retracing her steps, she found a root cellar on the far side of the house. A rusty padlock secured two wooden planks over the opening. She kicked at the lock and felt of a surge of elation when the aged metal broke open.

A creepy root cellar wasn't her preferred mode of entry, but she'd take it. Anything to get inside the Manor.

But what was she hoping to find?

Something…anything that might shed light on how Craig Taylor, Ray Sullivan and the still-missing Jason Wallace had been exposed to wasting disease.

Grabbing one of the handles, she tried to raise the covering. The weathered wood creaked in protest but refused to budge.

Repositioning herself for better leverage, she held her breath and pulled until her muscles strained with the effort.

Just when she thought her lungs would explode and her fingers rip from her hands, the plank broke free, sending her sprawling with a loud thud onto the damp ground.

"Yes!"

She scurried to her feet and peered down into the dark underbelly of the ancient structure.

What did she have to lose?

Okay, a lot. But if she didn't find the answers to her research dilemma, she'd lose even more.

With a quick swipe, she waved away a mass of spiderwebs and climbed down the stone steps.

The smell of damp earth and mildew filled her nostrils. Her lungs, still compromised from inhaling the smoke less than two days ago, tightened. She coughed repeatedly as she found the stairs leading to the first floor.

And hoped the door at the top would be unlocked.

Allison turned the brass knob and the door creaked open, exposing a dark, dank central hallway that ran the length of the antebellum house. Pulling in a reassuring breath, she walked toward the front door and into the office she'd viewed through the window. Her shoes clicked over the hardwood as she moved from there into the library across the hall. In both rooms, she eyed the extensive collection of books before she moved on.

A dining area, two classrooms and a kitchen completed the first floor. In the darkened upstairs, she found four more classrooms, and the steps to the stuffy attic, which had been divided into a series of rooms, each containing two bunks and a small wooden dresser.

Her footsteps echoed along the hall as she returned to the first floor and exited through the kitchen to the grounds in the rear. The first outbuilding was locked, and she peered in at what had undoubtedly served as a science classroom with black granite work areas and a hanging periodic chart.

Maps lined the walls of the second outbuilding, where a large globe was positioned in front of two rows of student desks.

Allison hurried down the overgrown walkway to the third building at the rear of the hedged enclosure. She pushed on the door, which unexpectedly opened, and she stepped inside, coughing as the musty air filled her lungs.

Ten desks were arranged in a circle in the middle of the room. A number of certificates and photographs decorated the walls.

She approached a black-and-white shot of a dignified gentleman with a gray beard and steel-rimmed glasses. Dressed in a pinstriped suit, he stood in the middle of the then richly embellished front office.

Professor Hightower perhaps?

Glancing quickly over the array of framed memorabilia, her gaze focused on a photograph, half-hidden behind a freestanding chalkboard.

Dirt and grime clouded the glass as well as the ever-tenacious cobwebs that hampered her view of the black-and-white glossy. Allison found a discarded scrap of notebook paper in one of the student desks and wiped it across the glass. Strands of spiderweb stuck to her fingers. She ran her hand over her skirt and glanced once again at the photo.

Her breath caught in her throat.

Five young men stood next to a live oak, where the carcass of a deer hung from a rope.

She squinted. Tall, black hair. Could that be a much younger and thinner Ray?

Pulling the frame from the wall, she held it close. And next to him?

"A clean-shaven Craig," she mumbled.

A guy who claimed he'd never hunted. Or at least his dad had mentioned he'd never owned a gun.

What about the other boys? Was one of them Jason Wallace?

Convinced she may have found the first thread of a connection, she tucked the photo under her arm.

A door creaked.

The hair on the back of her neck raised and her heart thumped hard against her chest.

Had the wind blown the door open? Or—

A footstep sounded behind her.

She grabbed a ruler off the nearby desk and twirled to face the intruder, brandishing the ruler like a weapon.

Her other hand flew to her throat.

Dark eyes. Raised brow. Hunting knife hanging from his belt.

"Luke?"

EIGHT

Luke saw the vulnerability play over Allison's face as her eyes flicked to the knife sheathed at his waist.

"Why'd you follow me here?" she demanded.

As strong as she was trying to be, fear edged her voice and that bothered him. The last thing he wanted was to frighten her.

"I saw you race out of the cabin. I thought you'd gone back to town to talk to Cooper."

"If you thought I was in town, why'd you end up here?" She clutched a framed photo against her chest, trying to appear in control, yet her eyes showed confusion.

How had they gotten to this point?

"Evidently you're like the townspeople who believed the gossip Cooper spread about me. Five minutes with him and you think I'm a killer."

She didn't respond, and her silence was telling.

Disappointment rose anew within him.

"You don't have to be frightened, Allison. We

haven't known each other long, but I thought you were someone who wouldn't listen to hearsay. Don't scientists focus on the facts?"

He stepped toward the door. "To ease your mind, I called the sheriff and asked if he'd seen you in town. He and Cooper were at the B and B, examining the fire damage. Vic hadn't noticed any cars headed toward Sterling. The only other logical destination was this school."

Opening the door, he glanced over his shoulder. "The manor's an aged structure. Some of the beams are rotten. I wanted to warn you about the danger."

He walked purposefully along the path and was almost to the back door of the main building when he heard her call his name.

"Luke, I'm sorry."

He turned. "A lot has happened. Maybe too much to sort out. But if you want to talk, come back to the farm. I'll put on a pot of coffee and brew some of that herbal tea you like."

Arriving home, Luke perked coffee and put the teakettle on the burner. He was relieved when tires crunched over the driveway, signaling Allison's return.

He hadn't realized how much he wanted— needed—her support.

"You jumped to the wrong conclusion," Allison said as she stepped into the kitchen. "I've never been afraid of you, Luke."

A weight lifted from his shoulders. "I should have told you about Hilary's death."

"And I should have talked to you before I raced out of here earlier."

He poured her a cup of tea and placed it on the table. "Bett and Shelly are working in the garden. You can ask me anything about that night."

She shook her head. "I don't need to. You've already told me what happened."

"But do you believe me?"

"You said Shelly saw it happen. Special children show their emotions readily. When she looks at you, Luke, her sweet face is filled with love. She trusts you." Allison pulled in a deep breath. "And if she trusts you, so do I."

It was what he'd been waiting to hear. They were back to where they'd been earlier that morning. Two people interested in getting to the bottom of a number of problems in their lives.

"What'd you find?" He pointed to the old photo she had placed on the table. Grabbing his cup of coffee, he stepped closer.

"That's Ray and the mayor's son."

"Do you know any of the other guys?"

Luke pointed to one of the teens. "That's Jason Wallace, Cooper's brother."

"What about the other two?"

"Most of the Manor students were from out of town. I went to college on the GI Bill after I served in the military and graduated that spring. I knew only the kids from town."

"Is the headmaster still in the area?"

Luke shook his head. "Professor Hightower was in his late sixties at the time. He had heart problems and passed away about six years ago."

"What about his wife and children?"

"They only had one child, a son. He died years ago but was survived by a daughter Professor Hightower and his wife raised as their own."

"So Hilary was the granddaughter's nanny?"

"That's right. The girl's grown now and moved away a few years ago, but Mrs. Hightower lives in an assisted-living complex about forty miles from here. I can give you directions."

Allison no longer needed his help so all he could do was offer her a listening ear, a place to stay and directions when she asked for them.

"Come with me, Luke. You know Mrs. Hightower. She'll be more apt to volunteer information if you're there."

Allison stared at him, her face open, her eyes accepting as she waited for his reply.

Did she realize what she was saying? "Are you sure you want my help?"

"As I told you last night, I've made my own share of bad choices. I'd be the last one to judge you. I need your help or I wouldn't have asked for it."

Allison wasn't afraid to speak her mind. He liked that.

There were other things he liked as well. She was inquisitive and a bit stubborn but in a good way. She'd come to Sterling, survived the fire and had readily accepted his family's friendship. Even when she knew the harsh reality of their past. Now she was asking for his help. How could he refuse?

He grabbed his keys off the table and stretched out his hand. "Let's go."

Without a moment's hesitation, she slipped her hand into his.

Luke's heart warmed. He'd closed himself off from people for so long. Being with Allison made him want to break down the walls of isolation he'd created to protect Shelly.

Or had he put those walls in place to protect the one secret he still carried that was too painful to share with anyone?

Even Allison.

The nurse's aide smiled at Allison as she and Luke entered the assisted-living complex and were shown into a fashionable parlor. Two couches covered in a textured jacquard and various side chairs in a companion fabric were clustered around a large brick fireplace. Gas logs blazed with warmth, adding a homey touch quite opposite from the institutional atmosphere Allison had expected.

FREE Merchandise is 'in the Cards' for you!

Dear Reader,

We're giving away FREE MERCHANDISE!

Seriously, we'd like to reward you for reading this novel by giving you **FREE MERCHANDISE** worth over **$20.** And no purchase is necessary!

You see the Jack of Hearts sticker above? Paste that sticker in the box on the Free Merchandise Voucher inside. Return the Voucher promptly ... and we'll send you valuable Free Merchandise!

Thanks again for reading one of our novels – and enjoy your Free Merchandise with our compliments!

Jean Gordon
Jean Gordon

P.S. Look inside to see what Free Merchandise is **"in the cards"** for you!

We'd like to send you two free books to introduce you to the Love Inspired® Suspense series. These books are worth over $10, but they are yours to keep absolutely FREE! We'll even send you 2 wonderful surprise gifts. You can't lose!

REMEMBER: Your Free Merchandise, consisting of **2 Free Books** and **2 Free Gifts**, is worth over $20.00! No purchase is necessary, so please send for your Free Merchandise today.

Steeple Hill Reader Service - Here's how it works:

Accepting your 2 free books and 2 free mystery gifts places you under no obligation to buy anything. You may keep the books and gifts and return the shipping statement marked "cancel." If you do not cancel, about a month later we'll send you 4 additional books and bill you just $4.24 each in the U.S. or $4.74 each in Canada, plus 25¢ shipping & handling per book and applicable taxes if any.* That's the complete price and — at a savings of at least 15% off the cover price — it's quite a bargain! You may cancel at any time, but if you choose to continue, every month we'll send you 4 more books, which you may either purchase at the discount price or return to us and cancel your subscription.

*Terms and prices subject to change without notice. Sales tax applicable in N.Y. Canadian residents will be charged applicable provincial taxes and GST. Offer not valid in Quebec. All orders subject to approval. Books received may not be as shown. Credit or debit balances in a customer's account(s) may be offset by any other outstanding balance owed by or to the customer. Please allow 4 to 6 weeks for delivery. Offer available while quantities last.

Mrs. Hightower's financial situation had to be sound from the looks of the upscale surroundings. Allison thought of the antebellum structure and the well-crafted furniture that still remained in the abandoned building. Surely Mrs. Hightower would have put the school and its furnishings on the market if money were an issue for her.

"Mrs. Hightower's lucky to be able to afford such plush surroundings," Allison whispered to Luke.

He nodded. "I'm glad things have improved for her. She helped her husband at the Manor and had to tutor kids at the county high school to make ends meet."

Before Allison could comment, a petite woman with upswept gray hair and an abundance of makeup shuffled in on the arm of an attendant. The staff member directed the older woman to a side chair.

"Call me before you start back to your apartment, Mrs. Hightower. I'll be right down the hall."

Her wrinkled face broke into a smile. "Thank you, dear. I'll let you know when I'm finished talking to my visitors."

She glanced at Luke, standing by the fireplace, and fluttered her hand in the air. "The staff is concerned about my blood pressure dropping too low and leaving me light-headed. Why, I took a fall just two days ago that still has me dazed."

Raising the glasses that hung around her neck, she twisted her head into the frames. With eyes greatly magnified by the thick lenses, she gazed first at Luke and then at Allison.

Luke stepped closer and introduced himself. "You knew my daddy, Earl."

The woman's smile widened. "High and I used to talk about the excellent job he did as sheriff. And I remember how proud your mama was of you."

She shook her head and tsked. "Terrible shame what happened to her. Sometimes life just gets too hard to live. I saw it with High." Her smile disappeared as her brow lifted. "Did you know my husband?"

"Yes, ma'am. Professor Hightower was a fine man."

Eager to ask the questions that played through her mind, Allison introduced herself and placed the photo in Mrs. Hightower's lap.

"I found this picture and wondered if you could identify some of the teens? I believe they attended Sterling Manor."

Mrs. Hightower stared for a moment at the photograph and then pointed to the tallest of the five boys.

"Why that looks like Ray Sullivan."

She adjusted her glasses. "And next to him is Craig Taylor."

Glancing up at Luke, she added, "You know your daddy and Craig's daddy used to be friends. I think it was hard for Monroe to see you do so well for yourself when his son—" She tilted her made-up face. "Well, you know Craig has problems."

"What about the other boys in the photo?" Allison encouraged.

The woman hesitated. "I'm just not sure."

Luke bent close and pointed to a third teen. "Don't you recognize Jason Wallace?"

Mrs. Hightower shook her head. "I'm afraid my memory's not as good as it should be."

Allison's heart sank. She had hoped Mrs. Hightower would provide the names of all the teens.

"But I do remember High considered the Wilderness Adventure Club his top priority."

"So the boys were members of the same hunting club?" asked Allison.

"That's right. Although I believe the club's focus was on camping, not hunting. My husband called them his high-maintenance boys. He believed outdoor challenges would give them a sense of accomplishment."

Allison thought of the campsite with the weathered cross. "Did they camp near the school?"

"Why, no, dear. They usually went to the West Point Lake area."

Luke looked at Allison. "Near LaGrange, Georgia. In the western part of the state."

"Ray would remember, if you talk to him. He and Dudley were best of friends."

Allison's neck tingled. "Dudley?"

"Dudley Cumming. An Atlanta boy. He's in the

picture." She pointed to the pudgy boy in the back row. "That's Dudley."

Mrs. Hightower hadn't been sure of Jason Wallace, a boy who had grown up in Sterling. Nor had she recognized Dudley when she'd first looked at the photo.

"Are you sure the boy's name is Dudley Cumming?"

"Why, certainly. Do you know him, dear?"

Allison didn't know Dudley Cumming.

But it was obvious from the photo the boys had bagged a deer on at least one occasion, which could have had wasting disease. If they'd eaten the venison or if they'd had cuts on their hands when they'd dressed the animal, she may have found the mode of infection.

Allison stared down at the photo still resting in Mrs. Hightower's lap.

Three men had tested positive. Now she knew a fourth person named Dudley Cumming was involved.

And the fifth boy in the photo? Could he be infected as well?

Before leaving the complex, Luke and Allison stopped by the receptionist's desk, where a nurse confirmed Mrs. Hightower had trouble remembering details from her past.

"Talk to her first thing in the morning, and she's as lucid as you or me," the nurse assured them. "By this time in the afternoon, things start to fade."

It seemed more than a coincidence to Luke that the three men Allison had come to Sterling to question had been members of the same club in high school. A club that had some involvement with hunting.

The current deer population was healthy, but what about when the photo had been taken?

Luke had served in the military and then had gone on to college. He didn't remember his dad mentioning a problem, and the game warden had assured him he'd never known of a case of wasting disease in Georgia.

"It has everything to do with that club," Allison said, as they headed south on the road back to Sterling. "Even if I disregard Mrs. Hightower's comments, the photo speaks for itself. The boys had bagged at least one deer. Now if I can just determine if they dressed or ate the venison, I may have the connection."

"But the boys' camping trip happened years ago, Allison. You told me you were concerned about the health of the current deer population."

"Wasting disease isn't spread by a bacteria or virus. The infectious agent is a prion, a protein particle that can lie dormant within the human body for years, even decades."

"So that's what causes the sickness in deer?"

She nodded. "Elk are also susceptible. The animals lose weight and waste away, hence the name. In humans it's called Creutzfeldt-Jakob disease, or

CJD, after two German physicians who first identified the condition. There's also scrapie in sheep."

"So every species has their own form of prion disease?"

"Not quite, although cattle are susceptible as well. Remember the mad cow disease outbreak in Great Britain?"

Luke had seen the video footage on the nightly news and suddenly realized Allison's concern. "That's why you need to identify the source of infection. If cattle were involved the problem would be widespread."

He thought of the meat-processing plants where one infected cow could contaminate ground beef shipped throughout the country. He also thought of the more than 250 head of cattle that grazed in the back pasture on his farm. The British outbreak had led to a massive slaughter of animals and major setbacks for the European beef industry. The disease would wipe out herds of cattle in the United States as well.

"Luckily the evidence points to Craig, Ray and Jason having been exposed by eating infected venison," Allison said.

Before Luke could question her further, she pointed to the Roadside Grill, which appeared in the distance.

"Do you mind stopping? I'd like to talk to Ray again."

Luke pulled off the road and held open Allison's

door as she stepped onto the gravel drive. The two of them then headed toward the restaurant.

The first of the early supper diners had parked their cars outside. Allison and Luke found Ray working in the kitchen.

Allison said a quick hello and then held up the photograph. "Do you know all these guys?" she asked, without giving him time to put down the knife he was sharpening.

Luke touched her arm and nodded at the restaurateur. "Hope you don't mind us barging in back here."

Ray dropped the knife on the counter and wiped his hands before he motioned for them to follow him into a small office across from the kitchen.

"We can talk in here." He pulled the door closed behind him.

Allison handed him the photo.

Ray nodded. "Craig Taylor and Jason Wallace. The other two guys are Dudley Cumming and Kendall Reynolds. We were all members of the Wilderness Adventure Club."

"You went on camping trips together while you were students at Sterling Manor?" Allison asked.

"Just about every month we'd do an overnight. The weeklong trips were held once a year during our fall break. That picture was taken our junior year, but that wasn't our deer. We met some hunter who had bagged his first kill of the season. Professor Hightower took our photo."

Allison moaned.

Luke understood her frustration. She needed to establish the route of infection. The pieces of her puzzle had started to fall into place. Now it seemed everything had been messed up again.

"What about your senior year?" she asked.

Ray paused for a moment and then nodded. "Professor Hightower got lucky our first day there."

"Who dressed the deer?"

Ray shrugged. "I don't know. I guess we all did."

"*All* meaning the five of you in the picture and Professor Hightower? Were there any other adults with you?"

"Sometimes the mayor would come along."

"Mayor Taylor?" Allison asked. "Did he help gut the deer?"

Ray wrinkled his brow. "Look, you'll have to ask him. Some of the details are a little fuzzy."

"I don't understand," Allison said.

"We were the troublemakers. Or so everyone used to say. Hyperactive, they called us. Today it'd be ADD or something or other."

"Attention Deficit Hyperactivity Disorder, ADHD," Allison volunteered.

"That's right. My medicine got messed up real bad that fall, and I ended up in the hospital right after the trip. 'Course that was when the school closed. Sorry I can't help, but I don't have good recall for most of that time. Maybe Craig Taylor can tell you more."

Allison glanced at Luke.

He nodded. "Let's go."

Leaving the restaurant, Luke heard someone call his name and spied Marcy taking a break out back.

"Give me a minute," he said.

Allison headed for the SUV. "I'll wait in the car."

"Don't mention this to Ray…" Marcy said as he neared "…but I heard Cooper Wallace tell Ray he's trying to get the sheriff to reopen that murder case."

The back of Luke's neck tingled. "Hilary's murder?"

"That's right. He said there's evidence that proves you're guilty. Something about a knife."

Luke's father's knife had come up missing after the murder. As far as he knew, the weapon had never been found.

"Did he specifically mention a knife?"

"He heard me in the kitchen and lowered his voice so I can't be sure."

"Why are you telling me?"

"You were nice to me in high school. Even when some of the guys made fun of where I lived." Marcy hesitated. "You told them to leave me alone so I figured I owe you."

Marcy had been the best of the bunch in her family. Despite an abusive father and a mother who had abandoned all of them, she had graduated high school and managed to survive on tips and the meager salary Ray paid her. Somehow she'd saved enough to buy a small house and take care of her younger siblings when their father had ended up in the state correctional facility.

"Thanks, Marcy."

"Just don't mention it to Ray."

After his dad's death, Luke had realized he couldn't trust Cooper Wallace. Ten years later and nothing had changed.

Cooper wasn't to be trusted back then. And he wasn't to be trusted now.

NINE

The real estate office was locked and the lights off when Allison tried the door. "Looks like they've all gone home for the night," she told Luke.

He pointed to the drugstore at the end of the next block. "Monroe might know where to find Craig."

Luke waited outside while a clerk directed Allison to the mayor's office in the rear of the store.

Glancing up as she approached, Monroe rose from behind his desk and extended his hand. "Good to see you again, Allison."

"I wanted to talk to Craig, but his office is closed."

"They're at a Realtors' conference in Rome, Georgia. Any way I can help?"

Once she mentioned the club and the fall trip Craig's senior year, Monroe smiled. "Sure, I remember. The weather was perfect, and the headmaster shot a deer the first day out."

Exactly as Ray had said. "Did the boys have

contact with the animal? Did they gut the deer, remove the innards, anything like that?"

"Professor Hightower wanted it to be a learning experience. He insisted I stand back and watch while the boys did the work."

"But you ate the venison?"

"That's right. Craig did as well." Monroe chuckled. "He was still a meat eater in those days. Seems to me he enjoyed the venison as much as any of us."

"Maybe I was mistaken, but when I talked to you earlier, I got the impression you didn't hunt."

"Actually, Allison, I said I'd never owned a gun. The headmaster was the outdoors enthusiast. He felt the boys should be exposed to hunting. Some would take to it. Others, like Craig, wouldn't."

The mayor pursed his lips. "After we talked, I did a little research on prion disease." He shook his head, his eyes filled with concern. "The thought that Craig might have a fatal condition scares me."

She held up her hand. "I told you the test is still in the developmental stage."

"But you think Craig was exposed either by handling the venison or eating it."

Allison had to pick her words carefully. "At this point, I'm just gathering information. Tell me, though, did you inspect the animal?"

"Healthy. Full coat. No problems, if that's what you're implying."

"An infected animal would surely show signs of

debilitation," she said, as much for herself as for the worried father.

"Then to solve this mystery, the next step seems obvious. Draw my blood. I was with the boys. I ate the meat. If infected game was the culprit, my blood will react like theirs."

Monroe had just offered her an opportunity to confirm her suspicions about the deer. "I keep a phlebotomy kit in my car, but it's at the Garrison farm. I could come back tomorrow."

"Nonsense. That would just delay things further. I've got syringes and needles in the pharmacy. Bet I can even find a tourniquet."

"I'll transfer your blood to the proper collection tube once I get back to the farm."

Allison waited as he searched for the necessary items. Much as she didn't want another person to be infected, if Monroe's blood tested positive, she'd have enough evidence to establish the source of infection and ensure the quarantined units would not be released for patient use.

Monroe returned with the necessary supplies, and Allison soon had the blood she needed.

"I'll personally run the test and let you know the results," she said before she left the pharmacy.

Although pleased to have things falling into place, she was overcome with the reality of what might lie ahead.

If more than one deer had been infected years

ago, other folks in Sterling could have been exposed as well.

She looked at Luke, waiting for her by the curb, then thought of Shelly and Bett.

Did that include the family that had taken her into their home? A family she was starting to care about in a very special way?

Once they arrived back at the farm, Allison explained the events of the past few days to Bett, starting with the test she was developing and ending with her concern the boys at the Manor had been exposed to infected venison years ago. Keeping the information as uncomplicated as possible, she was surprised by Bett's initial response.

"Why, Allison, dear, this just means we have to turn to the Lord and put our hope in Him."

No doubt about it, Bett's faith was strong. She'd given up her own dreams to help Luke raise Shelly and without regret. If only some of that hope-filled spirit would rub off on Allison. Right now she felt like a jumble of nerves. So much hinged on what happened when she returned to the lab to test the mayor's blood.

"The temperature's getting cool," Bett called to Shelly, who romped nearby on the driveway. "Play for a few more minutes before we go inside for supper."

The twinkle in Shelly's eye was encouraging, and her face was free of the strain that had been evident yesterday. Allison glanced from her to Bett and was once again struck by the strong family resemblance.

If she didn't know better, she'd think the older woman was Shelly's mother.

In her mind's eye, she saw the faded photo Shelly had retrieved from the stone fireplace. A photo of two pregnant women.

Allison pulled in a breath as the realization hit.

She looked at Luke. Did he know the truth? It seemed so obvious now.

"What do you think, dear?" Bett was waiting for Allison's response to a comment she had failed to hear.

"Pardon?"

"I told you we eat so much venison. We could all be infected. Sure would ease my mind if you tested our blood. Of course, Shelly's health worries me most."

Allison looked at Luke, who seemed less than enthusiastic about the idea.

Then he nodded. "Maybe Bett's right. If our blood tests negative, you'll know the present deer population isn't a problem."

Suddenly everything was getting too personal. Allison cared about the people in this family and about their future. Running a test on an anonymous specimen was easy. But when that specimen belonged to someone she was fond of…

She looked at Luke.

How *did* she feel? They'd only just met, but he'd saved her life twice in as many days. Surely what she sensed was gratitude and a deep bond of friendship.

Of course, she could collect a blood specimen from each of them. Luke was right. If they tested negative, she could more than likely rule out disease in the current deer population, and everyone would breathe a sigh of relief.

But what if the tests came up positive?

The thought sent a jab of fear into her heart. She'd deal with that when and if it happened.

Allison needed to return to her lab and run the specimens as soon as possible. It was up to her to find out the truth, and she felt the heavy weight of responsibility resting on her shoulders.

Turn to the Lord. Bett's words rolled through her mind. But could Allison trust God?

He'd ignored her cry for help years ago. Would He do the same again?

As serious as the situation was, maybe she *should* give prayer a try.

"Help me, Lord," Allison whispered, hoping no one else overheard.

After supper, she placed the box containing the blood specimens on the passenger seat of her car and climbed behind the wheel.

"I don't like the idea of you heading out alone," Luke said as he leaned into the open driver's window.

"It won't take me long to stop at the gas station

in town and fill up. While I'm doing that, you can help Bett put Shelly to bed. There's no reason to upset your sister's routine."

"Be careful," he warned.

"Luke, you're sounding paranoid. No matter what you think, I don't need an escort to Magnolia Medical."

He smiled and shook his head. "You are stubborn, but I'm still going to follow you to Atlanta. Although I think you should wait until morning to start out."

"That would just set everything back. I'm anxious to get the test run and ensure all of you are healthy."

"Then give me about fifteen minutes and I'll meet you at the bypass."

The drive to town was uneventful, and Allison soon had her car filled up, the oil checked and windshield cleaned.

She pulled onto the main road and switched her lights to high. As much as she'd tried to talk Luke out of following her to Atlanta, she was relieved she wouldn't be alone on the long stretch of lonely back road.

A sign warned of an approaching curve. Allison lowered her speed, anticipating the bend in the road. At the same time, she reached for the knob on her radio, hoping music would help to ease the emptiness she felt.

A melancholy blues singer filled the void but did little to curb the tingles of anxiety that washed over her when a flash of light filled her rearview mirror.

Where had the car come from?

The driver flicked his beams to high. She averted her eyes from the bright reflection and tried to focus on the road ahead.

The turn was sharper than she had expected. Allison strained to keep the car on the road.

Once again, she glanced in her mirror, this time blinded by the glare.

For an instant, she thought back to another night when lights had blinded her.

"Drew," she moaned, hearing the squeal of tires, the screech of brakes, the slam of crashing metal.

Her stomach roiled and a wave of nausea washed over her. Not now, not tonight.

She shook her head, sending the memories into the darkness.

The car pulled into the next lane and accelerated as it passed, then swerved back into the right-hand lane, cutting her off.

Allison pulled the wheel to the right. Her front tire left the pavement. She fought to regain the road.

The car—a black SUV—raced out of sight.

Allison coaxed her car to the shoulder and dropped her head into her hands.

Tears burned her eyes. She fought to hold them in check. She'd already cried too much for Drew, for her relationship with her parents, for a life filled with failure instead of success.

"Allison?"

She looked up as Luke opened the driver's door and pulled her into his arms. There in the security of his embrace she felt suddenly at home.

Luke drew a handkerchief from his pocket and wiped her eyes. "Tell me what happened."

She gave him a sketchy recap of the car that had passed, then cut in too close. "It was probably my fault, Luke. I should have lowered my speed even more going into the turn."

"I'm calling the sheriff."

"No." She pulled out of his embrace and shook her head. "I've caused enough trouble. Plus, I want to get back to Atlanta. Calling Vic will just delay everything longer."

"Are you sure you feel like driving?"

She smiled and swiped her hand over her damp cheeks. "I'll be fine as long as you're following me."

The drive to Magnolia Medical took five hours. Heavy fog brought traffic to a standstill and forced the highway patrol to close a section of interstate. He and Allison had sipped coffee at an all-night truck stop until visibility cleared.

Although he hadn't told Bett, he had shared Marcy's warning with Allison and his own concern Cooper might try to cause trouble. He wanted to get back to the farm as soon as possible. Once Allison ran the blood tests and had the results, he'd say goodbye and be on his way.

Not that he wanted to leave her, especially after her near accident outside of town. But she'd promised to return to Sterling after she talked to her supervisor about the boys' club and the questionable venison the members may have eaten.

At this late hour, the parking lot at the medical laboratory complex was nearly empty.

"A few techs staff a round-the-clock STAT lab," Allison explained. "Everyone in my area went home hours ago."

A cold wind blew as they hustled into the building and rode the elevator to the second floor. The tile floors gleamed with wax. The building was immaculately clean and appeared newly decorated.

Allison carried the box that contained the specimens she had collected. Luke had worried Shelly would be upset about having her blood drawn, but he'd underestimated the woman walking next to him. His heart had warmed with appreciation when she'd turned it into a game of whose blood could fill the tube the fastest.

Shelly had eagerly extended her arm and watched with fascination. While there had appeared to be little difference in the rate of blood flow between the three of them, Allison had declared Shelly the winner and had rewarded her with a special princess bandage.

He smiled at the memory as their footsteps echoed in the hallway. Allison stopped in front of a door bearing a biohazard logo and the words Special Projects Laboratory. Authorized Personnel Only. She swiped her name badge along a keypad and punched in a security code.

A steady hum from a row of refrigerators welcomed them, along with a faint odor of chemicals. Allison led the way through a maze of rooms filled with large freestanding automated instruments and computer terminals. Sturdy laboratory benches topped with black granite provided a number of workstations where tall-backed stools sat in front of microscopes, now vacant.

Allison hustled toward an area in the rear of the lab with a large automated machine perched on the countertop. A maze of color-coded plastic tubing threaded through various testing blocks on the analyzer, like lanes on a freeway.

Placing the cardboard box on the counter, she grabbed a disposable lab coat from the closet and held out one for Luke. The paperlike material crinkled as he slipped his arms through the sleeves and snapped the front closed.

A box of gloves sat on the counter. She slipped her hands into the protective latex and handed a pair to Luke.

"Hey, I'm just an observer." He laughed.

"But you might touch something, and I don't want you exposed to anything hazardous."

"Are you referring to my blood specimen?" He pointed to his chest and widened his eyes with exaggeration, trying to make light of something that was far more serious than he wanted to admit.

"You're funny," she deadpanned.

Suppose one of them tested positive?

The thought sent concern slithering down his spine. No, he wouldn't consider that possibility. He was convinced the deer population was healthy. At least, he could vouch for the animals he had seen on his property and in the surrounding woods.

What about the venison Bett sometimes bought from the various food lockers? Surely they could trust their neighbors in Sterling to be vigilant as well.

But he didn't trust them when it came to other things, now did he?

Allison's movements were sure as she popped off the red rubber stoppers from the four tubes of blood, reamed the coagulated specimens with a disposable wooden stick and dropped the tubes into a small centrifuge.

The hum of the revolving tubes filled the lab, making it hard to converse, so he watched in silence as she proceeded to the next part of the test.

"Looks complicated." He raised his voice over the mechanical whirr.

"It's a fairly straightforward test. The centrifuge separates the blood into serum, buffy coat and—"

When he held up his hand, she stopped her explanation and smiled.

"You don't need to know how it works, just that it does the job. Right?"

He laughed. "You got it. Too much scientific talk, and I'm lost. Fact is, I'm already lost. Just let me know when the test is over."

Allison pointed to a stool. "The procedure itself is rapid, but the preparation is lengthy. Why don't you sit there, and I'll get everything rolling."

He dutifully did as he'd been instructed. From that vantage perch, he could focus just on her. The view was good, and he enjoyed the subject matter.

Amazed at the care Allison used in setting up the procedure, Luke realized his former opinion of medical personnel had changed. Allison's work required concentration and attention to detail. She was a determined and committed professional in every way.

At long last, she pushed a large button on the front of a machine and waited until it chugged into operation. Slipping off her gloves, she threw them in the trash and motioned him into a small break room.

Luke followed her lead, relieved to have his hands free of the confining latex.

"Coffee won't take long to perk." She filled the carafe with water and poured it into the back of the enclosed system. "There should be some apple pie in the fridge and a batch of brownies. Unless they've all been eaten."

"You baked?" Luke opened the refrigerator and reached for the dark-chocolate bars.

"Are you kidding?"

She laughed, and he liked the sound. In fact he was beginning to like everything about this scientist who had come into his life just forty-eight hours earlier.

"I bought the brownies at the local bakery. But they're delicious."

He could smell her perfume, no longer aware of the chemicals in the air.

She was standing close to him. Close enough for him to notice the way her eyebrows arched expressively over her blue eyes and the soft swell of her lips.

Close enough to know that he needed to keep his mind focused on the reason they'd driven through the night to get to Magnolia Medical.

If what Allison had said was true, three people were infected with a fatal disease. In the next fifteen minutes or so, he'd know whether his sister and aunt had been exposed as well.

He needed to think of anything except the way he wanted to hold Allison in his arms.

As Luke devoured two brownies and gulped down a cup of coffee, Allison pulled a phone book from the cabinet and opened it on the counter.

"We've got a few minutes while the test runs. Maybe I'll get lucky and find a phone number for Dudley Cumming," she said.

"Mrs. Hightower said he lived in Atlanta, but that was years ago. He may have moved away by now."

"You're right. But you never know." Her finger worked down the page. "Here's a D. W. Cumming who lives in Marietta." She jotted down the number on a scrap of paper and stuck it into her purse. "I'll phone him in the morning or, better yet, stop by and see him face-to-face. Body language can be so telling."

She looked up and caught Luke staring at her as he leaned against the counter, legs crossed at his ankles and a crumb of brownie dangling from the corner of his mouth.

The look in his eyes made her breath catch. She glanced away, caught off guard.

He straightened and stepped closer.

Her hand lay on the phone book. His fingers touched hers. A delectably warm sensation swept over her, something yummy and more delicious than the sweets in the refrigerator.

"Excuse me," she said. "But you've got—"

She pointed to his face with her free hand.

Luke's cheeks colored in a boyish way that charmed her and contrasted sharply with the longing that filled his eyes.

She brushed her fingers against his lip, knocking the crumb free and hurling her heart into over-drive.

"I was so worried when I saw your car on the side of the road." His voice was thick with emotion as he moved even closer.

She inhaled the scent of him, a fresh masculine smell that hinted of the outdoors.

The muscles in her neck tensed.

"Luke, I…"

A buzzer rang from her workstation.

"Saved by the bell," she mumbled.

Neither of them moved.

Caught in time, she soaked in his nearness and the overwhelming strength of him before she forced her mind back into lab mode. She needed to read the results.

Luke followed her to the workstation, where she removed the plastic covering from the reaction tray.

He hovered close by. "Well?"

She studied the reactions. "No doubt about it. You're all negative."

"Thank God." He sighed deeply. "And Monroe?"

"He's negative as well."

Her feeling of elation plummeted. "The mayor said he ate the venison, but he wasn't involved when they dressed the animal. The answer lies somehow in the gutting. Either that or I've been following the wrong lead."

Luke's cell phone rang. He glanced at the caller

identification before he flipped it open and pulled it to his ear.

"Allison just got the results of the test. I'll put you on speaker so she can tell you herself."

Bett's voice amplified through the lab. "Tell me it's good news."

"You and Shelly and Luke tested negative," Allison quickly reassured her.

"Thank the Lord, and I do mean that literally. I've been praying all night. Hate to tell you, Luke, but it looks like we've got more trouble ahead."

"What's wrong?"

"Vic called. He wanted to warn us."

"Has Cooper Wallace been throwing his weight around?"

"Worse. He wants the murder case reopened. Vic tried to ignore his demands, but an anonymous informant phoned the sheriff's office last night, claiming there was incriminating evidence hidden on the farm. The call came from a payphone in Atlanta."

"Probably someone Coop hired to make the call."

"Vic's hands are tied. If he doesn't do something, Cooper threatened to bring in the federal authorities."

"That's nonsense."

"Cooper knows a lot of people in government. Vic said the best solution is to let him handle it. He needs a search warrant. That'll take time. Cooper's trying to speed the process along. I told Vic you were in Atlanta with Allison. He said to hightail it back home as fast as you can."

"Tell Vic I appreciate his letting us know."

"You'll need help with Shelly," Allison said once he flipped his cell closed. "I'll follow you in my car."

"You have to talk to your boss about the blood units, and you wanted to stop by the Cummings' home."

"I can talk to both of them by phone."

She glanced at the Jewett refrigerator. "But first I have to ensure the three units aren't inadvertently released for patient use."

She walked purposefully toward the large glass front refrigerator, opened the door and pulled the quarantined units into the crook of her arm. After checking the unit numbers and the fluorescent orange tags printed with block letters that read DO NOT TRANSFUSE, she kicked the refrigerator closed and placed the units next to the sink.

"What are you doing?" Luke asked.

"Making sure no one becomes infected from this blood."

She grabbed a pair of surgical scissors and three large ziplock plastic bags and placed a unit in each of the bags.

"Didn't your daddy ever tell you about weighing the consequences before you act?"

"I'm already in trouble, Luke. My funding is gone, and the board doesn't seem convinced my procedure is valid. I've run out of time, but I've never felt more right about anything."

She snipped off a corner of the donor units to ensure they would not be released for transfusion and then zipped them within the sturdy plastic storage bags.

Turning to the nearby computer, she typed out a detailed explanation of what had happened and why.

"Veronica will access her e-mail as soon as she arrives at her office. I wanted her to know why I tampered with the units."

Allison dropped the three plastic ziplock bags containing the positive units into a cardboard bio-hazard container. Grabbing a black indelible marker, she wrote For Test Purposes Only in large letters across the top of the box, then placed it on the bottom shelf of the small reagent refrigerator, far from the huge Jewett, where the blood for trans-fusion was kept.

"This way, I'll still have the blood samples to evaluate after all this is over. Undoubtedly, the board will hold an investigation to review my actions and determine whether I should remain at Magnolia Medical."

The first light of dawn glimmered on the horizon as they left the building and headed for their cars.

"Say a prayer things will work out," Allison said as he opened the door for her.

"We'll both pray on the way back to Sterling."

"No, Luke, we need a prayer now."

Taking her hands in his, he said, "Lord, Allison wants assurance You're in control, and as messed up as things seem, I do, too. Help us in the day ahead. Protect us from harm and protect those we love."

She squeezed his hands before she slipped behind the wheel. "Let's get out of here. Something tells me we're both in a lot of trouble."

TEN

Luke pulled into his drive exactly two hours and forty-five minutes after he'd left Magnolia Medical. Allison parked directly behind him.

The sheriff's car sat in front of the house along with three other cars, all belonging to law enforcement.

Bett raced to greet them. "Vic and his deputies got here about thirty minutes ago."

Luke nodded to the sheriff. "Looks like you're getting an early start."

Vic leveled a tired gaze at Luke. "I doubt either of us got much sleep last night."

"Bett told you I drove back to Atlanta with Allison."

The sheriff acknowledged her with a nod as she stepped from her car. "You still trying to get to the bottom of those blood tests?"

"That's right." She moved to where Bett stood. "Where's Shelly? I'll take her over to the cabin to keep her calm."

"They're searching the cabin at this very minute.

Besides, she's in her room and refuses to come out."
Bett wrung her hands, her face drawn.

"What do you expect to find?" Allison demanded
of the sheriff.

Before he could answer, a deputy opened the
cabin door. "I found a couple photos shoved behind
a loose rock in the fireplace." He crossed the
driveway and handed the pictures to the sheriff.

"Those belong to Shelly." Allison stepped forward.

Vic looked at both photos, then turned questioning eyes to Bett. Her hand flew to her mouth.

"I don't see how they would be of interest to
anyone," Allison insisted.

Evidently the sheriff agreed. He placed them in
her outstretched hand.

"Sorry for the inconvenience."

As if things couldn't get worse, Cooper Wallace's Town Car pulled into the drive.

"Glad to see you're cracking down on this case,
Sheriff," the lawyer said as he climbed from his car.
"Should have been done ten years ago. Would have
been except your predecessor tried to protect his son."

"Get off my property." Luke fisted his hands,
having difficulty controlling the anger that swelled
within him.

"You can't be serious." Cooper pointed to Luke
but focused his eyes on the sheriff. "Vic, tell him he
has no right—"

"Head back to town, Coop." The sheriff's voice

was firm. "Let the authorities handle things for a change."

The lawyer's eyes narrowed. "Any more comments like that and your job may be in jeopardy."

"Yes, sir. I hear you. Now get in your Town Car and get going. I'll call you if I have a problem."

Cooper opened his car door, then paused when a deputy emerged from the barn.

As he neared, Luke realized he was carrying two see-through evidence bags.

"Found some things hidden under the floorboards in the feed room," the deputy told his boss.

Vic held out his hand and took the bags.

"It a Garrison hunting knife, sir. E.G. is carved into the handle. Must have belonged to Luke's dad."

Luke stepped closer. "That knife's been missing for years."

"And the other bag?" the sheriff asked.

"Blue work shirt, sir. Size extra large. The initials written in the collar are L.G."

Luke stared at the cotton shirt.

"Both items appear to be stained with blood," said the deputy.

The sheriff turned to Luke. "You want to explain?"

Over the years, Luke had owned work shirts that looked identical to the one the sheriff held. His father had a number of them as well. "I don't know anything about the shirt or what's on it."

He stared at the other evidence bag. Unlike the

shirt, he recognized the knife that had belonged to his dad.

Cooper stood by his car. "It's probably Hilary's blood. You need to arrest him."

"Shut up, Cooper." The sheriff nodded to Luke. "We better go down to my office and talk things over."

At that moment, Shelly ran from the house. The gut-wrenching sounds that swelled from deep inside her tore through Luke.

She stumbled down the steps and threw herself into his arms.

"It's okay, darling," he soothed, trying to console her.

"Time to go," the sheriff said.

Luke glanced at Bett for help with Shelly, but she seemed too dazed to notice his need.

A hand brushed his. Luke turned. Allison stood beside him, her eyes filled with compassion. "I'll take her."

Slowly, he nudged his sister into Allison's embrace. She pulled Shelly close and rubbed her hands gently across the girl's back.

"Luke has to talk to the sheriff for a while. He won't be gone long. Bett and I'll take care of you, honey."

Guilt welled up in Luke. He should have tried to get to the bottom of what had happened that night in the clearing. Instead he'd holed up like the recluse he'd become. Now, after all these years, he'd have to confront something that had haunted him for so long.

The sheriff took Luke's arm and guided him toward the squad car.

Shelly continued to moan, while Allison whispered soothing words of comfort.

His sister couldn't understand what was happening. All she knew was that her brother—her closest kin—was being taken away by the sheriff.

No wonder she couldn't be consoled.

Allison held her tight against her heart as Luke climbed into the rear of the sheriff's car. Bett slumped into the porch rocker, her face as pale as death.

Cooper Wallace pulled onto the main road, heading back to Sterling. Behind him the lights flashed from the sheriff's car.

Luke glanced out the rear window, a thick lump wedged in the back of his throat.

How had everything turned so wrong in such a short time?

Allison ushered Bett and Shelly into the house and sat them at the kitchen table while she fixed breakfast. Eggs and toast. Under the circumstances, she'd forgo the sausage.

The smell of perked coffee filled the kitchen. She poured a cup for Bett and milk for Shelly.

"I hardly feel like eating." The older woman sighed, toying with her food.

Shelly looked up, her eyes troubled.

"It's okay, child. Sheriff Vic won't keep Luke long." Bett gave her a reassuring smile and rubbed her hand over Shelly's shoulder. "Eat your breakfast and don't worry."

Shelly did as she was told, seeming to find comfort from Bett's closeness.

"Cooper Wallace is behind this," Bett insisted. "I wouldn't put it past him to have planted the knife and shirt in the barn."

"You're sure the knife belonged to Luke's dad?"

"I told you the Garrison family tradition. Every male makes his own knife. Earl treasured his and kept it in a special box over the mantel. Until he found Shelly playing with the empty box outside."

"Luke told me what happened. Amazing how similar the knives are. The one they found today looks just like the knife Luke carries. You said he manufactures them now?"

"The knife the deputy found belonged to my brother. I saw the initials on the handle. Doubt there would be another one like it. The manufactured pieces are good, but they're mass-produced. Anyone knowledgeable about hunting would know the difference."

"Did you recognize the shirt?"

"Every man who works with his hands has a shirt like that. Luke has had plenty of them over the years. So did Earl. They're pretty common for folks in the country."

"And the stains?"

"They could be anything."

Shelly raised her head and glanced at Allison, who stood by the stove.

"It's okay, honey."

She tried to reassure the girl, but the tone in her voice revealed her own concern. Had someone hidden the knife in the barn? Or had Luke's dad found the evidence long ago? Was that the reason he had taken his own life?

Allison's phone rang. She retrieved it from her purse and her gut tightened when she saw the name on the display.

"Veronica, I can explain what happened."

"Not over the phone." Her supervisor's voice was controlled but stern. "I'll expect you in the lab within the hour."

"But I drove back to Sterling this morning. Even if I left now, considering traffic at this time of day, it would take me more than three hours. Plus…"

How could she explain what had happened? A family that had reached out to her was caught in the twisted grip of scandal. Worse than that, the man who had saved her life was a suspect in a brutal murder.

"It looks like the donors ate infected venison while on a camping trip," said Allison.

"Can you can trace the infection to the venison?"

"That's what I'm trying to do. You told me the board had questions about the quarantined units. I couldn't take the chance they might be released for transfusion."

"You destroyed laboratory property."

"I'm well aware of what I did."

She glanced at Bett and Shelly, who were both watching her, their faces reflecting the concern Allison felt.

Bett grabbed Shelly's hand and bowed her head. "Oh, Lord, help Allison at this moment with whatever problem she's facing. We need her to stay with us here in Sterling."

Gratitude filled Allison, sending renewed resolve coursing through her veins.

"Veronica, I know you think I was out of line, but we're talking about a fatal disease. I consider my actions justified under the circumstances. Give me a little more time to sort everything out. I will get to the bottom of this problem. And if I'm wrong, I'll reimburse the laboratory for the destroyed blood units."

"You know the bill will be high."

And her present bank account wouldn't cover the cost, but somehow she'd find a way. "I'll pay it back over time."

"The board wants a report in twenty-four hours."

"But—"

"No buts. Twenty-four hours. The clock's ticking. You're into the countdown."

Allison knew it was useless to ask for more time.

"And one more thing," Veronica added. "The board contacted your dad."

Her stomach tightened. "What?"

"They've been searching for a guest lecturer to speak to our research department. Your father said he'd be happy to talk to the group about the lab's role in monitoring surgical patients. He plans to be here next week. I'm sure he's looking forward to seeing you."

The phone went dead. Exactly the way Allison felt. Once again, her father would know she had failed.

Twenty-four hours.

It had to be enough time. But was it?

Allison helped Bett tidy up the kitchen after breakfast. They dried the dishes and put them away in the cabinets, before Allison mentioned she needed to drive to town.

"You go on," Bett insisted. "Shelly and I will spend the day in the garden. Being out in the fresh air and working with the soil calms her as much as it does me."

"You really are so much alike," Allison said.

Bett let the dishwater out of the sink and dried her hands on a towel before she turned to face Allison. "You know, don't you?"

Allison looked at Shelly with her red hair and facial expressions that mirrored Bett's. "Only after I saw the photo."

Bett followed Allison's gaze. Shelly sat at the table intent on cutting pictures out of a stack of old magazines. Her fingers struggled to control the blunt school scissors that protected her hands from mishap.

"I left Sterling when I graduated high school," Bett said, "determined to make a name for myself in the big city. Only I could hardly earn enough money waiting tables to pay for my room and board."

She sighed. "I turned my back on my family. On my family values as well. I was too big for my britches, as my daddy would have said if he'd lived long enough. Luckily he never knew what happened to his firstborn."

Allison patted her arm. "You don't have to explain anything to me, Bett."

"But I need to admit the truth to myself. Luke's not the only one who's been a recluse all these last years. I'm at fault, too."

She placed the dish towel on the counter and leaned against the refrigerator, hidden from Shelly's line of vision. When she spoke her voice was low so only Allison could hear.

"Just before I hit rock bottom, I met a man who said he loved me." Bett shook her head ever so slightly. "He said a lot of things and none of them were true. Things about commitment and being together for the rest of our lives."

"You were young and alone," Allison offered.

"And stupid," Bett quickly added. "Not only had I turned my back on my family, but I'd turned my back on God as well."

The conversation was hitting a little close to home in Allison's opinion.

"I forgot—or chose to forget—about a loving Father whom I could turn to in time of need. Instead I shut Him out of my life and ran in the opposite direction. Right into the arms of a man who told me nothing but lies."

"What made you decide to come back to Sterling?"

"Desperation. He wiped out my meager bank account, took my pride and anything of value I still owned and left me alone and ready to deliver a child he didn't want." She wrapped her arms around her waist. "At that point, I wondered if life was worth living."

Allison touched Bett's shoulder. "But you came home."

"Thanks to a woman in the neighborhood. A do-gooder, as we used to call her." Bett smiled at the memory. "She found me on the street with nothing and drove me home to Sterling. I'll be eternally grateful to her and to my brother Earl and sister-in-law Miriam, who welcomed me back."

"Miriam was pregnant."

"That's right. She was due a couple weeks after me, but she went into labor almost thirty-six hours before I did."

"And her baby?" Allison asked, fearing the worst.

"Was stillborn. The midwife who delivered both of our children did her best."

"You didn't go to the hospital?"

"It was seventy-five miles away and the onset of labor was fast. Miriam never would have made the trip. And I didn't want people to know what a mistake I'd made of my life."

"That's why Earl and Miriam said Shelly was their baby," said Allison.

"Earl came up with the plan. He thought raising my child as their daughter would force Miriam out of her grief. But she never recovered and died three months later."

"By then you were caring for Shelly full-time."

"People said I loved her as if she were my own. Only they didn't know the truth."

Allison glanced at Shelly. A stack of coupons in a variety of shapes lay scattered about the table.

"Didn't Luke realize what had happened?" asked Allison.

"He was overseas and didn't come home until after I delivered. Shortly after that, he left for college."

"It might ease some of the burden Luke carries to know whose daughter she really is."

Bett furrowed her brow as Allison continued. "He feels a great sense of regret that he hasn't been able to protect Shelly. That's a heavy load to carry."

"I don't know if I'm ready to tell him."

Allison patted Bett's arm, understanding her hesitation.

"Best I pray about it," the older woman said.

When she'd arrived in Sterling, Allison hadn't believed in the power of prayer.

Now the idea of a loving God was gaining merit. Luke and Bett must be rubbing off on her.

ELEVEN

Allison had a lot to think over on the way to town, especially her rather tenuous position at Magnolia Medical. If the board's investigation proved her wrong, she'd lose her job.

Being fired would be a red mark on her record. The medical community was small and news spread quickly. She doubted any other lab, especially any reputable research lab, would be interested in hiring her after word of what had happened circulated.

The realization saddened her, yet the contaminated units needed to be removed from the inventory. Mistakes happened even in the best of medical facilities. She couldn't have forgiven herself if an error had occurred.

No, she'd made the right decision. Although she'd never be able to explain that to her father. She'd continue to meet her mother in the city for lunch, but any type of reconciliation with Dr. Stewart would be out of the question.

A sense of loss settled heavy on her shoulders as she drove into Sterling and passed the town square. The sheriff's office stood on the next block. She glanced at the building, wishing she could see Luke. But there was nothing she could do to help him at that moment, and she needed to talk to Jason Wallace.

Pulling in front of the Wallace campaign headquarters, Allison rummaged in her purse and found the scrap of paper with D. W. Cumming's phone number. Might be wise to talk to Dudley—if the number proved to be his—before she faced Jason.

Tapping the digits into her cell, Allison counted six rings and was ready to hang up when a woman answered.

"Mrs. Cumming?"

"Who is this?"

"Ma'am, I'm trying to locate Dudley Cumming, who attended Sterling Manor a number of years ago. I wondered if this might be his number."

"Dudley's my son. But he doesn't live here anymore."

Allison gave her name. "I work for a medical laboratory in Atlanta, and I'm doing some research on the students who attended the Manor."

She wasn't sharing all the information, but she didn't want to alarm the mother with talk about a deadly disease. "Could you give me his current phone number so I can contact him?"

"I've got your number on my caller ID. I'll tell Dudley to contact you when he gets back to Atlanta."

"He's out of town?"

"And won't be back for another month. He's in charge of a South American project for his company. Unfortunately, it's a remote site so I can't reach him by phone."

No telling what would happen in the next month. If only she could encourage the woman. "Your son was a member of the Wilderness Adventure Club. Did he ever talk about Kendall Reynolds?"

"Why sure. Dudley and Kendall were good friends. They kept in touch until he died about six months ago."

Allison pulled the phone closer to her ear. "Do you know how Kendall died?"

"All I know is he had seizures and a disease the doctors couldn't identify."

"What about a number where I could reach his family?"

"Dudley might be able to help you when he gets back."

"Mrs. Cumming, I hate to keep questioning you, but the information is important. I wonder if you recall anything about the fall campout of your son's senior year?"

"I'm not sure I should give out information over the phone."

"I understand. I have to be back in Atlanta tomorrow. May I stop by your house so we can talk in person? I'd be happy to bring you my credentials. I work for Magnolia Medical."

"I'm aware of their excellent reputation. Unfortunately, I'm flying to Houston tomorrow to visit my daughter." The woman paused and then sighed. "I doubt it would hurt if we talked for a minute or two. Of course I remember that campout. They closed the Manor right after the fall break. My husband was alive then, and we ended up placing Dudley in a private school here in Atlanta."

"Did he talk about the campout?"

She laughed, her previous inhibition seemingly gone. "Only that he didn't like venison and never wanted anything to do with hunting."

So much for Professor Hightower's desire to expose the boys to the outdoors.

"It sounds like Dudley's done well for himself. You must be very proud of your son."

"Oh, I am. He's turned into such a fine, upstanding young man. Of course, we had our share of trouble with him early on." Mrs. Cumming sniffed. "If you're researching the school, you must be aware the Manor was for boys with behavior problems. The headmaster promised we'd see improvement. I must say Dudley *was* different when he came home that fall."

"Different?"

"After the school closed, he was—" she paused

"—more subdued. Maybe it was the therapist we found who finally seemed to connect with him. The counseling sessions helped. He let Dudley talk. Evidently, all sorts of tall tales came out. You know boys."

"Anything you can remember about the camping trip per se?"

"Hmm. Campfires and swapping scary stories about wild animal attacks." The woman chuckled. "Dudley had a few issues about cleanliness. I remember it bothered him that their jeans and shirts were so badly soiled they burned them in a bonfire before they came home."

Allison was glad Dudley had overcome his behavior problems, but she was painfully aware of the medical condition that would impact his future.

"Then there was the poison ivy," Mrs. Cumming continued to ramble. "Worst case he's ever had. No wonder the way his hands were."

Allison tightened her grip on the phone. "What about his hands?"

"Evidently, they'd made a game out of searching for food. I forget what they ended up finding. Blackberries maybe. Anyway, he got a terrible case of poison ivy because of all the cuts on his hands. Went right into his bloodstream the doctor said."

If Dudley had had cuts on his hands, maybe the other boys had as well. Mrs. Cumming may have provided the very clue Allison needed.

Now, if only Jason Wallace would be as forthcoming.

* * *

"Allison just drove into town," the sheriff announced, glancing out his office window.

Luke looked up as her car edged out of sight. "She wanted to talk to Cooper's brother this morning."

"About that deer problem? Persistent, isn't she?"

"She believes in what she's doing."

"Shelly's taken to her from what I saw this morning."

Luke thought again of how his sister had cried in Allison's arms. The memory tore at him.

"How long before you'll hear back from the crime lab?" Luke asked, frustrated to be holed up in the sheriff's office.

"They'll call when they've finished the initial tests. Could be another hour. Could be all day."

"Maybe I should contact a lawyer," Luke said, eyeing the man he'd always considered a friend. "And I'm not talking about Cooper Wallace."

"I told you, Luke, it's your decision. Like I explained earlier, I'm trying to appease a loudmouth politician who can do more harm than good. Let me work this the way I planned, and I'll get you home for supper if not before."

Luke owed the sheriff his gratitude. If it had been someone else's watch, he could have been under lock and key. Vic had allowed him to sit at one of the deputy's desks in a side office. He'd shoved a

Bible into his hands and suggested he seek comfort from Scripture to pass the time.

Luke opened the leather-bound book, hoping God would speak to his heart.

"Be still and know that I am God." The message the Lord had given the Hebrews during their captivity. Wise words then. Equally sage now.

He'd bide his time and wait until the sheriff had the lab results he needed. Barring any unforeseen circumstances, Luke would be home with his family tonight.

Shelly. Bett. Allison.

Allison? When had he started to think of her as family?

Be still. The words echoed in his mind. The Lord would answer his questions in due time.

And what about his heart? There were questions that needed to be answered in that regard as well.

"Thanks for meeting with me."

Allison placed her notebook on the table in campaign headquarters and settled into a straight-backed chair opposite Jason Wallace. Although tall and good-looking, he lacked the affected air she'd noticed in his brother.

"Cooper said you've been away on business for the past couple days," she began.

"That's right. I was lining up some appearances for him in the Augusta area."

"Certainly is a beautiful spot. Did you drive over to the coast?"

He smiled. "Unfortunately, I didn't have time. I headed back through Atlanta and picked up I-75 south of town."

So Jason had been in the greater metro area yesterday when someone had called the sheriff's office from an Atlanta payphone. She wouldn't put it past Cooper Wallace to convince his brother to make that call.

Luke had said he couldn't trust Cooper. What about his brother?

Pulling in a deep breath, Allison ran through the same explanation she had given both Craig and Ray about her reason for being in Sterling. When she finished her spiel, she showed him the photo of the five boys.

A wide grin settled over his face. "Takes me back, you know what I mean?"

"I'm sure it does. Do you remember your last camping trip with the group?"

"Fall of our senior year. Right before the Manor closed."

"I understand you guys ate a lot of venison."

"A bit. Professor Hightower shot a buck the first day."

"And you dressed the deer?"

"Hightower and the mayor did most of the work."

"The mayor? Are you sure?"

"Yeah, why?"

Because the mayor had remembered the details differently. "I understand you scavenged for blackberries."

"We ate our fill of those back at school. You ever see the Manor's backyard?" He chuckled. "Besides, it was fall. Berries weren't in season."

Allison ran her fingertips over her own hands and thought of the natural barrier the bushes provided.

Jason glanced at his watch. "I'm not sure where all your questions are headed, Miss Stewart, but I've got another appointment." He started to rise.

"Of course. I know you must be busy."

The door opened and Cooper Wallace stepped into the office. Surprise registered on his face when he saw Allison.

"I thought you'd be out taking care of that handicapped Garrison girl while her brother's in jail."

She bristled. "The sheriff is questioning Luke. He's not under arrest."

"That'll change once the crime lab identifies the stains on the knife and shirt."

Allison didn't want to talk to the obnoxious politician. She grabbed her purse and notebook and headed for the door.

"He's fooled you, Allison. Fooled all of us in Sterling." Cooper's voice followed her into the outer office, where a number of people were stuffing envelopes with campaign flyers.

"Luke Garrison is a murderer," he shouted after her. "Watch your back. We wouldn't want another woman to die in Sterling."

Allison hoped to find the mayor at the drugstore. Instead she found Craig, rifling through papers on his father's desk.

"Dad said you drew his blood. Did you get the results yet?"

"You can let him know he doesn't have to worry."

"Meaning I *do?*" Craig picked at his chin.

"At this point, it's hard to say. I talked to some of the other guys who were in the Wilderness Adventure Club."

Craig nodded. "Dad said you quizzed him about that last campout we took."

She'd quizzed all of them about a camping trip that should have been the highlight of their young lives.

The most important question was how they had been exposed to the infectious wasting disease.

"Craig, tell me about the scratches on your hands."

He widened his eyes and dropped the pencil. "You saw something in my blood that came from the blackberry bushes?"

She hadn't mentioned blackberries. "Where were the bushes?"

He shrugged and tried to backpedal. "In the woods, of course. We were camping for a week. Cuts and scratches happen."

She couldn't get a straight answer from anyone. Maybe she ought to try a different tactic and see where it led.

"A woman I know in Atlanta enjoys refurbishing old homes. I drove by Sterling Manor yesterday and wondered if the owner would be interested in selling the property. Should I talk to Mrs. Hightower?"

He shook his head. "Wouldn't do you any good. A friend of Dad's owns the place. He lives near LaGrange. I could contact him and see if he wants to sell."

"The same man whose land you camped on?"

"That's the guy."

"Professor Hightower must have told your father about his plans to start a school."

"Dad put the two men together, if that's what you mean. Professor Hightower wanted to open a school where he could test some of the theories he'd picked up when he was in Europe. Only problem was, he didn't have the cash."

"And your father had the resources?"

"That's right. Plus he thought I'd do well in a small, private school." Craig smiled but his eyes were filled with regret. "Truth was, I'd always been a disappointment to him."

Craig's honesty surprised Allison. She knew what it was like not to live up to a father's expectations.

"Can you tell me anything about Professor Hightower's theories?"

Craig shrugged. "Only that they didn't work on me."

Ray had talked about being hospitalized, and Dudley Cumming had needed extensive therapy once he'd returned home to Atlanta. The headmaster's nanny had been brutally murdered not far from the school, and two other people had died on a neighboring farm.

Not the type of environment she'd want for her child.

"Tell your dad I was looking for him," Allison said as she left the pharmacy.

A woman who had tutored kids to make ends meet, living in a posh complex for seniors, might provide more information.

If she was having a good day.

And if not?

At this point, Allison had nothing to lose and everything to gain.

"I thought you might stop by," the sheriff said.

Leaving the Bible open on the desk, Luke stepped into the front office and smiled when he saw Allison.

A warm tingle spread over him despite his frustration at being forced to stay put in the sheriff's office. "Vic saw you drive by earlier. I was worried you might run into Cooper."

Allison shook her head in amazement. "The guy's about as hospitable as an ant."

Luke bristled. "What did he say to you?"

"He made some comments about you. That's what I didn't like. Not that I stayed to hear it all. But he did mention waiting for the crime-lab report."

Allison looked at the sheriff. "Surely you're not holding Luke until the results come back? It might be days before they even begin to process the evidence. And if you're waiting for a DNA test, that could take until after the New Year."

"Blood type is what I wanted. The results should be back by close of business."

Luke glanced at his watch just as he had done every few minutes since he'd first arrived in Sterling.

The phone rang. "This might be the call we've been waiting for." The sheriff raised the receiver to his ear and sighed. "Now, Bett, I told you when you called last, we're still waiting on the crime lab." He paused. "I understand it's hard on Shelly."

Luke let out a sharp breath. "Is she okay?"

The sheriff held up his hand and nodded.

"I know. You're right, of course."

Sounded like Bett was giving the sheriff a piece of her mind.

"Yes, Bett." He glanced at Luke and shrugged. "That won't be necessary. Allison just stopped in. She can drive him home."

The sheriff hung up and chuckled. "Shelly's fine, but that aunt of yours is a determined woman."

Luke smiled despite the circumstances. Seemed Bett's persistence had paid off.

"Mind giving me a ride home?" he asked Allison.

The sheriff wagged his finger at both of them. "Make sure you stay at the farm and away from Cooper. I don't want him getting riled up again. The man can cause trouble you and I both don't need."

Luke extended his hand. "Thanks, Vic. I owe you."

He shook his head. "No, you don't, son. Your daddy was about the best man I've ever known. You're his equal. That means a lot in my book."

Luke appreciated the comment.

Once they were outside, Allison tossed him the keys. "Think we can take a little detour? I need to talk to Mrs. Hightower again."

"I'll call Bett, and let her know it may take us longer than expected to get home."

"Tell her we're together," Allison said.

Luke liked the sound of her voice and liked her comment about being together. Being with Allison felt right.

In fact, despite everything that had happened today, a spark of optimism ignited within him. Maybe they could get to the bottom of Allison's investigation as well as his own. Once the problems were behind them, they'd be able to consider what the future would hold.

"I'm hoping Mrs. Hightower might be more alert this time of the day," Allison said. "I have less than twenty-four hours before I need to be back in Atlanta."

Luke's enthusiasm plummeted. Allison's research was important to her. Why would a city girl who was making a difference want to trade a career in medicine for a quiet life in the country?

He had allowed his thoughts to wander too far astray. Allison would leave Sterling tomorrow.

Where would that leave him?

Alone.

Not where he wanted to be.

TWELVE

Allison saw Luke's neck tighten as he glanced in the rearview mirror. "Looks like we've got company," he said.

She turned around and spotted a blue Town Car. "Cooper?"

"From the make of car, I'd say yes, although I can't see who's driving because of the tinted windows."

The Town Car accelerated.

"Hold on. I don't like the way he's gaining on us."

Allison braced her hand against the dash.

Luke pressed on the gas, and the speedometer crept higher.

"The road intersects up ahead. Straight would take us to the assisted-living complex. I'll veer right, then turn onto a dirt road that parallels the paved two-lane. We may be able to lose him."

A four-way stop loomed in the distance. Luke slowed enough to maneuver the curve, then accelerated. Luckily some of the leaves were still on the trees, concealing their route of escape.

"He's not behind us anymore," Luke said once they crested the small hill. At the bottom of the downward slope, he turned into a deeply forested path and cut the speed.

Allison glanced out the rear window. What would they do if the Town Car followed them?

"Cooper seems to have this personal vendetta against you, Luke. What caused it?"

He shook his head. "A bit of jealousy, I guess."

"Did it involve Hilary?"

"Cooper had dated her a couple times the summer before she died. I'd graduated from college in June and moved back home the following month. Hilary and I went out a few times, nothing more."

"So you didn't steal her away from Cooper?" Allison couldn't help but tease.

"Hey, cut me some slack. She told me Cooper had been less than a gentleman. According to Hilary, she'd never given him reason to think there was anything between them."

Allison thought of the picture she'd seen. Hilary was an attractive woman. No wonder Luke had been interested.

"Did anyone suspect Cooper after her death?"

"He had an alibi, but that didn't stop him from spreading lies about me. He said Hilary and I had argued. That I'd threatened her."

"Your father didn't believe him?"

"My father never talked about the investigation. He didn't even share his thoughts with Vic."

"Everyone assumed you murdered Hilary before you drove back to town."

Luke turned to stare at her. "And changed clothes in the barn where they found the shirt this morning. Is that what you're thinking?"

She looked into his eyes. As strong as he was, she saw his need for reassurance. "I told you before, I know you're innocent."

He exhaled the breath he'd evidently been holding.

"It's time to move on, Luke. Let's head to the assisted-living complex so I can talk to Mrs. Hightower."

The old lady's eyes were clear and her complexion rosy when they found her sitting in the front reading room.

She remembered their names and acknowledged them with a warm welcome. Evidently, she was having a good day.

"You look just like your father," she told Luke, who beamed at the comment. "I was sorry to hear he took his life."

The smile on Luke's face faded. "He died from a gun accident, Mrs. Hightower."

Her eyes widened behind her thick lenses. "Is

that what happened? You know I saw him the night he died. He came to talk to High."

"Are you sure about that?" Luke asked.

She fluttered her hand. "Of course I'm sure. He pounded on the door about eight-thirty. I had just finished in the kitchen. High was on the phone. When I answered the door, your father hardly had two words to say to me before he charged into the living room. Said he needed to talk to my husband in private and closed the door after himself."

"Do you know what they discussed?"

"Probably the camping trip. High had been away with the boys." She shook her head. "The 'troubled ones,' as he called them. Although they were important to him. Maybe more than the others."

"Did it have to do with the theories he'd heard about in Europe?" Allison asked, remembering what Craig had mentioned.

"High thought the boys—his high-maintenance ones—would help establish him as an expert."

"Dealing with youth who had behavior problems?" Allison offered, trying to find her way through the old woman's ramblings.

"That's it exactly. High had learned so much, but his experiments were risky."

Allison glanced at Luke. "What type of experiments?"

"Why, his experiments with drugs to modify bad behavior."

A pinprick of anxiety crept along Allison's neck. "What type of drugs?"

"I can't remember, dear. It's probably in his book, *Handling the Hyperactive Child.* You can find a copy in the library."

Allison glanced at the books lining the shelves of the cozy reading area.

"Not this library, dear. The one at the Manor. I know there's at least one copy. High dedicated the book to our son. He had problems, like the troubled boys. That's why High became so interested in altering behavior."

She looked at Luke. "You understand, don't you? With your sister and all."

Luke let out a frustrated breath.

"Did Monroe Taylor contact you about starting the school?" Allison asked, hoping to get Mrs. Hightower back on track.

"Yes, he was worried about his son. We were raising our granddaughter in Germany at that time. Hilary worked for us, and when High received Monroe's offer, we asked her to come with us."

The old woman pursed her lips. "Hilary cared for you, Luke. And she seemed especially fond of your father. Did she tell you she had planned to go back to England?"

"Yes, ma'am. She told me."

"England?" Allison looked from Luke to Mrs. Hightower. "I thought you lived in Germany?"

"We started out in England. That's where we met Hilary."

"Excuse me, Mrs. Hightower, but it's time for bingo," an aide said as she stepped into the room and helped Mrs. Hightower to her feet.

At the door, the older woman looked back at Allison.

"Such a shame about Hilary. Broke High's heart, you know. Mine, too, when I called her parents. They'd just lost their son." She tsked. "He was only a year older than Hilary."

"Had he been ill?" Allison asked.

"Seizures, as I recall. The mother said a number of people in England had similar symptoms. Perhaps my granddaughter remembers more of the details. She keeps in touch with them."

Mrs. Hightower patted the aide's arm. "Her phone number is in my address book. I'll have Nettie get it for you."

Once Allison had the number in hand, she and Luke raced to the car.

Silence hung between them as Luke drove back to the farm. He was focused on the past. And Allison? Probably thinking about the future.

She planned to leave town in the morning.

Not that Luke would stop her. He knew she needed to get back to her research.

When they arrived at the farm, she excused herself to make a phone call and scurried into the cabin.

Wouldn't be long and he'd hear from the sheriff. If the crime lab eventually determined the blood on the shirt and knife was Hilary's, Luke could have serious problems on his hands.

Why, Lord? He'd tried so hard to isolate himself and Shelly and Bett from the past. Ten years. He'd succeeded until Allison had crashed into their lives.

If they hadn't been driving along the road that night, they never would have…

What was he thinking? He never would have saved Allison from the flames. He never would have held her or felt his heart thump with excitement whenever she entered a room.

The sheriff was right. He had been hiding out from life. Not really living all these years. Had he been afraid to face the reality of the past? What was it he was worried he'd find?

That his father had been involved with Hilary? Mrs. Hightower had implied as much.

He'd seen Hilary talking to his dad late at night after Luke had said good-night.

She had been a few years older than Luke. Attractive. His father had been alone for six long years at that point. Of course he'd be interested.

Why else had he had been so secretive, not even letting his deputy in on the investigation?

The clearing was a special spot where his dad

had loved to build a bonfire and sit for hours, watching the twilight settle into night.

Hilary had complained of a headache so Luke had dropped her at the cabin. Had she gone to the clearing, hoping to find his father? Instead, she'd found a murderer who had taken her life.

When Luke had called for help, his father had arrived at the house within minutes. Yet he'd told Luke earlier he'd be on patrol in Sterling. Had his dad planned to meet Hilary at the clearing but arrived too late?

Luke had never tried to get to the bottom of the heinous crime because of concern for his father's memory. Now, his back to the wall, he had to sort it out.

Heavyhearted, Luke climbed the steps to the porch and found Bett in the kitchen. She pointed to the table.

"Sit down, Luke. Shelly's resting in her room, and we need to talk. There's a secret I've been keeping from you about my child."

As soon as Allison entered the cabin, she pulled her cell from her purse and tapped in Mrs. Hightower's granddaughter's phone number.

After attesting to the older woman's health and good spirits, Allison said, "I'm staying with the Garrisons, in fact in the same cabin where Hilary lived. Your grandmother and I talked about how much she meant to you."

"That's a painful chapter in my life."

"Which I can fully understand. Mrs. Hightower said Hilary was from England."

"That's right. She lived in Stratford near where my grandfather was teaching when we first moved to the U.K."

"Do you know anything about her brother's illness?"

"Only that it was some type of degenerative neurological disease. Last I heard, her father was having similar symptoms. If you'd like to talk to the family, I have their phone number."

Once Allison jotted down the number, she disconnected and tried the international exchange, frustrated when no one answered.

She'd try again later. Right now, she needed to stop by the Manor and find the copy of Professor Hightower's book his wife had mentioned.

If she could trust the woman's memory.

Peering out the window, Allison saw Bett and Luke sitting at the kitchen table. Hopefully, she was telling him about Shelly. The last thing Allison wanted was to disturb them.

She glanced at her car and weighed her options. If she tried to drive, Luke would probably be outside before she started the engine.

The school wasn't far. Surely she could walk.

Her mind flashed to the Town Car that had followed them earlier. Cooper didn't frighten her, but she didn't want to face him again today. Better to skirt the road and take the path through the woods.

Of course, then she'd have to worry about the aggressive buck. What were the odds she'd see the same animal twice?

Just to be safe, she grabbed the shears from the desk drawer and dropped them into her pocket. They offered little to no protection, but the weight of them filled her with a sense of security.

Okay, a false sense of security. But at least it was better than nothing.

Besides, if she hurried, she'd be back before anyone knew she was gone.

Setting off along the path, Allison heard a screen door slam. She turned long enough to see Shelly step onto the porch. Before the child could notice, Allison slipped behind a large oak.

She didn't want Shelly following her into the woods the way she'd followed Hilary so many years ago.

Luke shook his head when Bett finished talking. "Why didn't Dad tell me Shelly was your daughter?"

"Would it have made a difference?"

Luke wasn't sure.

He looked into Bett's weary face. She had come back home, like the "prodigal daughter," pregnant and alone, and his parents had accepted her back with open arms.

What would have happened if his biological sister hadn't died? He'd never know. The baby *had* died. And his parents had accepted Bett's child as their own.

That didn't affect the way he felt about Shelly or his aunt. He loved them dearly and wanted the very best for both of them.

The phone rang and Bett answered, then handed him the receiver. "It's Vic."

"They called with the results," the sheriff said when Luke got on the line.

"And?"

"It's human blood. B positive. The same as Hilary's blood type. They'll run DNA to confirm if it's hers."

"I didn't do it, Vic."

"The lab determined the shirt had been laundered repeatedly, yet the initials had been freshly applied onto the fabric with an indelible marker."

"Someone wanted it to look like my shirt."

"Seems that way."

Luke told the sheriff about the incident with the Town Car.

"I'll talk to Coop. If he wants to call in authorities from the state level, so be it. But I'm the one in charge of this investigation right now. Stay put, Luke. I'll keep you posted."

Luke's feeling of relief when he hung up was quickly replaced with agitation when he glanced out the window and spied the blue Town Car with tinted windows pulling into the drive.

Cooper Wallace. The last person Luke wanted to see.

He stepped through the living room and headed for the front porch, ready to give the lawyer a piece of his mind for following them earlier.

At the speeds they had been going, anything could have happened. If Allison had been hurt, he never would have forgiven Cooper or himself.

Just as always, he held on to his anger. Something his father had told him was a personal weakness.

Mule-headed, his dad had called him. Maybe he was.

Right now he planned to show Cooper just *how* mule-headed he could be.

THIRTEEN

Allison stared at the wooden cross that marked the spot of Hilary's death. A lump formed in her throat as her mind ran helter-skelter with various scenarios.

A vagrant camper? Someone from town? Cooper Wallace?

She shook her head, sending the thoughts scattering. Her goal was to find Professor Hightower's book. She couldn't be distracted. Not even by the grim reality of death.

Racing along the path, she soon reached the Manor. Once again, the cellar provided entry. Ignoring the musty smell of the damp earth, she climbed the stairs where the door hung open.

Hadn't she pulled it closed yesterday? Maybe the wind had blown it free.

An uneasy quiet filled the house. Allison didn't have time for nervous jitters. She stuck her chin in the air with determination and headed for the library.

The heavy brocade curtains hung open, allow-ing the late afternoon sun to filter into the room. She neared the bookcase and ran her eyes over the spines of books neatly arranged back-to-back before she moved on to the office. Her footsteps echoed along the expansive hallway.

The wind picked up outside, and a current of air whistled down the main stairwell. Long shadows danced across the walls.

She glanced out the window. Dark clouds rolled across the sky.

She needed to hurry.

Her gaze fell past the desk to a stack of books propped up on a nearby table. She read the titles. Nothing by Hightower.

A corner shelf proved equally discouraging.

Where else had she seen books?

Now she remembered. Hurriedly she raced out the back door. Thunder rumbled overhead.

Without an umbrella or raincoat, she'd be soaked before she made it back to the farm.

Scurrying along the stone walkway, she arrived at the farthest outbuilding and stepped inside. The photographs lining the walls stared back at her.

A bolt of lightning crisscrossed the sky.

Her eyes darted to a small shelf in the corner and a bound manuscript. *Handling the Hyperactive Child,* by Hudson Hightower, Ph.D.

Flipping open the cover, she read the dedication: "To my son, Jackson, my wife, Ethel, and to Monroe

Taylor, without whom this project could never have been realized."

So the mayor had been involved.

Allison tucked the book under her arm and retraced her steps across the enclosed backyard.

Entering the school, she dashed along the central hallway to the front door. Before she touched the brass knob, the door opened.

Luke stepped onto the porch. Bett stood behind him in the doorway. "Careful, Luke. The sheriff told you to watch yourself."

The driver's door opened, and the lawyer climbed out of the car. Aviator sunglasses covered his eyes. He slipped them off and dropped them into his breast pocket.

"What do you want, Cooper?"

"Just checking to see if you made it home."

"So now you're the self-appointed escort service from town? I didn't appreciate you following me earlier."

"And I didn't appreciate you racing away. I wanted to talk to you."

"If you've got something to say, now is as good a time as any."

"We've been friends since we were kids in school."

"That's past tense, Coop. You made your decision ten years ago."

"I was young and thought I was in love. You

always seemed to get the girls. I was hurt Hilary chose you instead of me."

"You told people I killed her."

"I didn't know what to think. You'd been with her that night."

"So you spread lies about me. About my family."

"You had everything, Luke, that I wanted. A home you could be proud of, a loving dad. My family was the laughingstock of town. A drunk for a dad. A mother who liked men more than she cared about her two kids. No wonder my brother had so many problems."

"We don't pick our families. Folks in town knew that."

"Easy for you to say. Seems they were always pointing their finger. I wanted them to point it at someone other than me."

"You got what you wanted."

"I had a talk with Jason this afternoon after Allison left his office. Evidently he might have some type of rare disease. Jason's worried. So am I."

"That's why you followed us?"

"Jason's all the family I have now. I need to know what's going on. Is she here?"

Luke turned to Bett. "Let Allison know Cooper wants to talk to her."

Bett tapped on the cabin door, then pushed it open and looked inside.

"She's gone."

Pinpricks of concern tightened Luke's chest. "Where's Shelly?"

Leaving Cooper outside, Luke raced into the house, calling Shelly's name. When she failed to answer, he climbed the stairs two at a time and searched the second floor.

Bett met him at the foot of the stairs. "Could she have gone off with Allison?"

"First, I'll check the barn."

He thought of the gun storage area. Surely the deputies would have locked the case after their search.

Luke ran faster than he ever had. The cabinet was filled with hunting rifles. The ammo was kept in a separate box, all locked. If the deputies had secured the padlock.

Please, God.

His stomach tightened.

Dark clouds floated overhead, hiding the late afternoon sun.

Hold off the storm, Lord, until we can find Shelly.

He shouted her name as he approached the barn. "It's Luke, honey. Your—"

What was he now? Her cousin? He'd always been her brother. No matter what, he'd always be there for her.

"It's Luke, honey. Your brother. Where are you?"

He pushed on the barn door and raced into the darkened interior. Hay, feed and farm implements, but no Shelly. He ran to the storage area in the rear. The room where his father had died.

The gun case stood in the corner, padlocked shut. He yanked on the metal lock to ensure it held tight. Shelly couldn't have gotten into the guns or ammo.

But if she wasn't here, where was she?

And where was Allison?

Allison's hand flew to her neck and a gasp escaped her lips.

"I've scared you." Monroe Taylor stepped into the Manor and closed the door behind him.

Allison took a step back and pulled in a few deep breaths until her heart slid back into a more even rhythm.

"I didn't expect anyone to be at the door," she said.

"Of course not." His eyes played over the book she held clutched in her hand. "I keep the house locked up. How'd you get in?"

"Through the cellar."

"Looking for something to read?"

Allison's cheeks burned under his steady gaze.

He held out his hand. "May I see what you've taken?"

"Borrowed," she corrected him. "I'll bring it back tomorrow."

"The book, Allison."

"It's the text Professor Hightower worked on

while he was out of the country. Isn't that why you invited him back to Sterling?"

Monroe raised an eyebrow. "I invited him?"

"That's right. It was your idea to start the school. Because of your son, no doubt. Was he having trouble? Perhaps with the law? I'm sure it's difficult to watch a child make bad choices with his life."

The words spilled out of Allison's mouth before she could weigh whether giving vent to her thoughts would be wise.

She was tired and frustrated and needed to get to the bottom of everything that was happening. Somehow a woman's death, this strange school and three men who had been infected with a prion disease were all wrapped up together.

"You have no idea how hard it can be for a parent," Monroe moaned. "Especially when your son's the town fool. I have a nice home and am well thought of in the community. Craig should have been one of the exemplary students, like Luke. But my son had problems. Inherited from his mother's side of the family. She was no good from the start. Leaving him when he was a child was proof of that."

Allison wondered if the woman had left or been forced away by a husband who had demanded her to be something she wasn't.

"So you thought a special school would help Craig?"

"High had a new theory. Stimulants were being

used to calm hyperactive children with some success. He took that to its logical extreme."

The threads were starting to weave together.

She tapped the book she still held in her arm. "Experimental drugs. Is that what Professor Hightower claimed would help Craig?" She flipped open the pages. "He probably mentions the specific drugs in his book."

It didn't take her long to find the list of medications. Phencyclidine?

"Surely he wasn't experimenting with PCP?"

Monroe grabbed the text from her. "One of many he was convinced would work."

"Only he didn't have authorization to distribute the meds, and he couldn't find a physician who would write a prescription for drugs that would cause more harm than good."

She glared at him.

"Without a doctor's authorization, the professor couldn't implement his theory, so that's where you came in, isn't it?"

Monroe's face tightened. "You're jumping to the wrong conclusions."

"Am I? You own the only pharmacy in town. Did you provide the illicit drugs to the school?"

"That would be unethical, and I'd lose my license."

"Especially if it were revealed that a heinous crime had occurred while the boys were under medication."

Monroe shook his head. "You're wrong."

"Hilary was killed not far from here. Easy enough for a group of drugged-up boys to sneak out. What'd they do, find her in the woods?"

"Don't you think the sheriff considered that very possibility and dismissed it when he learned the boys were hours away on a campout in LaGrange?"

"You and Professor Hightower were the chaperones, but you didn't drive to LaGrange until later that night. After you realized the boys had committed the crime."

She pointed her finger at his chest. "The truth is, you were in Sterling when Hilary died. Luke saw you rush out of your store after you'd received a phone call. Did Professor Hightower call to tell you the boys had snuck out?"

"Dad?"

Allison turned to see Craig standing in the doorway from the basement.

"What are you doing here?" Monroe demanded.

"Learning about what happened that night. You told me the nightmares weren't real. That I'd heard about Hilary's death and internalized what had happened." Craig's eyes clouded with confusion. "All these years and you let me believe I was imagining my own involvement."

"Craig, please. Leave this to me."

"Like everything else. You always try to help, but invariably you make things worse for me. You never believed I could take care of myself. You had to set me up with the real estate firm, but you never let me make decisions of my own. I told you Professor Hightower was giving us drugs, and you told me not to worry. I didn't know you were the one supplying the pills."

"I was trying to help you."

"You were trying to help yourself. I was an embarrassment to you then, just as I still am. The fact is, you can't stand weakness in anyone else. That's why you ran my mother off. She was never good enough for you."

"You don't know a thing about her."

"I did a search for her on the Internet. We've been e-mailing back and forth for a number of weeks. She told me how things were."

"You can't believe her."

"I can and I do. Because I know how you've manipulated my life all these years."

"We have worse things to worry about." Monroe grabbed Allison's arm. "She'll expose everything."

"You can't keep covering up, Dad. You know everyone else had left school that day, except the five of us in the Wilderness Adventure Club. The high-maintenance kids as Professor Hightower used to call us. We were supposed to wait until you got off work and closed up the store. But when Professor Hightower went home to get his gear, we got into the meds. It was Jason's idea. He was always the ringleader of the group. He said he'd found special pills that would pull us out of our lethargy and make us stronger and smarter. He even said you'd be proud of me."

"He tricked you, Craig."

"I didn't know anything most days with the medicine Professor Hightower forced us to take. Didn't you realize it, Dad?"

Car tires sounded on the pavement outside. Monroe looked out the window. "It's Jason. What does he want?"

"I told him to meet me here," Craig said. "I wanted to get to the bottom of this once and for all. I thought if we came back to the Manor, I might be able to separate fact from fiction."

"You're a fool," Monroe raged. He pulled a roll of duct tape from his pocket, tossed it at his son and shoved Allison forward. "Tie her up while I talk to Jason."

Craig shook his head. "It's too late, Dad. Jason said he remembers what happened that night."

Monroe grabbed the tape from his son's hands. "Give me that. I'll do it, just like I've always had to do everything."

Allison gasped. "You killed Hilary."

"She was dead when I found her," he insisted. "The only thing I had to do was make it look like she'd been killed with Garrison's hunting knife. I'd taken it away from that crazy daughter of his one day when she'd strayed onto the Manor property. Served him right for keeping the knife where she could find it."

Allison tried to run, but he grabbed her arms and twisted them behind her. "You don't scare easily, do you?"

She cried out as pain cut through her shoulders. "What do you mean?"

"The night I cut the power in the cabin. With all your talk about a blood disease, I knew you'd stir up trouble. Did you really think I hadn't kept up-to-date on prion disease? Hilary had told Hightower about her condition so I used gloves when I handled her body, but I feared Craig might have been infected."

Monroe wrapped the thick tape around her wrists and legs.

"What are you doing?" She struggled to be free.

"Making sure you won't cause any more problems."

She turned her head to look at Craig. "You said your father takes care of everything, but it costs you in the long run. Don't let him do this."

Craig picked at his chin, confusion written on his face. "I can't stop him."

"Of course you can. Don't you see what he did to you? He made you kill Hilary."

"That's not true." Jason opened the door. "We all killed her."

"Shut up," Monroe said.

"We snuck out and headed for the clearing in the woods to build a fire and get an early start on our camping adventure. The pills started to work. Next thing we knew a wild animal was coming toward us through the underbrush."

Allison moaned. "You thought Hilary was a wild animal?"

"I told you, it was the drugs," Craig cried.

"Your dad's to blame," Jason said, pushing Allison aside.

She fell to the floor, hitting her head against the floorboard. The room shifted around her. She blinked, hoping to clear her vision.

Jason had Monroe by the shoulders and slammed a fist into his gut.

The mayor doubled over. "You don't know what you're doing."

"That's what Cooper tells me. But he thinks it's the pot I smoked as a kid. He doesn't know it's because of the drugs you filled us with at this school."

"Lay off him," Craig demanded, grabbing Jason's arm.

He turned, swung and hit Craig on the tip of his pointed chin.

Monroe screamed as he watched his son crumble to the floor.

Jason threw another punch. This one sent the mayor crashing against the office door. His head smacked the doorjamb. Lunging forward, Jason jammed his fist into the mayor's ribs. Monroe groaned, then collapsed next to his son.

Grabbing the tape, Jason wrapped it tightly around both men's arms and legs. "They're not going anywhere."

"What are you doing?" Allison fought to free herself.

He kicked her in the stomach, knocking the air from her lungs.

Jason ran outside. A car door slammed, and a caustic smell filled her nostrils. Gasoline.

Allison gasped. "*You* started the fire at the B and B."

"No one told me anyone was staying upstairs. Cooper had taken out a large insurance policy on the old structure. It was in both our names. I needed cash, only he didn't want to sell the place."

"You set the fire so you could collect the insurance?"

"And I would have succeeded, if you hadn't come to town and started throwing your weight around. You brought everything out into the open."

"It was because of your blood specimen. I wasn't sure until I realized you and the other boys in the club had murdered Hilary. She was from England, where a prion disease called CJD was running rampant. Did you ever hear of the mad cow disease outbreak? Infected cattle passed the disease on to unsuspecting consumers who ate the beef. Only they didn't get sick immediately because the infectious prion lies dormant within the human body."

"Mad cow? I saw it on the news a long time ago. The cattle couldn't stand up."

"It affects the central nervous system. You scratched your hands when you crawled through the blackberry bushes and headed to the clearing."

"The professor had locked the front door and we couldn't get out except through the rear," Jason admitted, looking down at his hands as if remembering that night.

"When you bludgeoned Hilary, her blood entered your bloodstream through the scratches on your hands. Her brother had died just before she was murdered, and her father is having problems now. Hilary had the disease although her symptoms were just starting. Ray said she'd been having severe headaches. Remember Kendall Reynolds? He died six months ago."

Jason hesitated, and Allison knew the truth. "You're having headaches, aren't you?"

He shook his head.

"What about seizures, double vision, memory loss, depression?"

"I'm fine. The only thing I need to do is get rid of you. Then everyone will still believe Luke killed Hilary with that knife of his dad's. They say that's why the sheriff committed suicide. He couldn't face the truth."

"Monroe tried to cover up the crime you boys committed. He stabbed Hilary after she was dead, hoping to throw the blame on Luke. Yesterday he hid the knife and the shirt he'd been wearing in Luke's barn. Then he had you call the sheriff when you drove through Atlanta."

"The newspaper reports never said she'd been bludgeoned."

"Luke's dad had been concealing that information, hoping to expose the person who had committed the crime. He must have suspected the truth because he visited Professor Hightower the night he died. The professor warned the mayor. He killed Luke's dad to keep him quiet and made it look like suicide. Turn yourself in, Jason. The judge will take into consideration that you boys were on medication."

Jason shook his head, a wild gleam in his eye. "I don't believe you."

"Call Luke and tell him what happened. He'll help you."

"I'm smart enough to solve my own problems. You're just like Cooper, thinking you can push me around. I'll show you."

Jason backed out the front door.

Allison heard a match strike and the whoosh of fire.

Twisting her head, she saw him race to his car and drive out of sight.

She saw another car parked in the drive. A black SUV. The mayor had been the person who tried to drive her off the road the night she'd headed to Atlanta.

Allison strained to free herself. The scissors were in her pocket, but as much as she tried she couldn't reach them.

Staring into the growing flames, she knew if the Lord was ever going to hear her, it had to be now.

"Lord, you're my only hope."

FOURTEEN

"Shelly, where are you, honey?" Bett's voice sounded from the garden area. Seeing Luke, she ran toward him as he neared the house. "Cooper drove back to town. He'll let us know if he spots her along the way," she said.

"Shelly wasn't in the barn and the weapons are still locked. I'll head along the path to the clearing. Maybe she went that way."

"Oh, Luke. Surely she wouldn't have gone back there."

"Not unless she was following Allison."

"Take your knife. You might need it." Bett placed it in his outstretched hand.

Luke slipped the knife onto his belt and took off running. He had to find Shelly. And Allison.

He called both their names as he raced along the path.

Lord, I've made so many mistakes in my life.

Forgive me. And help me make things right in the future. Give me another chance with Shelly, with Bett and, most of all, with Allison.

Allison closed her eyes, seeing her brother Drew, her father and mom. The people she loved.

A vision of Luke floated through her mind and an overwhelming sadness overtook her. She and Luke needed more time together to build on their relationship.

She'd never felt as connected to anyone else in her life, not even Drew. Yet she and Luke hadn't been given enough time. Was that by God's design?

She shook her head. God didn't bring problems to the people He loved. Hard times were a by-product of this life and the bad choices people made.

Had coming to Sterling been a bad choice?

Once again she saw Luke's smiling face. Shelly stood next to him. No, coming to Sterling had been good for all of them.

A groan sounded behind her. Allison jerked. If she didn't know better she'd think... She shook her head. The crackle of the fire was affecting her hearing.

Another groan. Could it be?

She turned her head and saw Shelly standing wide-eyed, her hand on the basement door.

At her feet lay the two unconscious men.

"Oh, Shelly, did you follow me here? You need to run and get help. Find Luke."

The girl shook her head. Stepping around the men, she dropped to her knees next to Allison.

The flames licked at the front door. Smoke filled the front hallway.

"You've got to get out of here. Go back home."

"Arrgh." Shelly tugged at Allison's arm as if trying to pull her along the floor, but the task proved too daunting.

"You can't save me."

The girl shook her head. Tears ran from her eyes.

"Get Luke." Why couldn't she make her understand?

Shelly grabbed Allison's wrist and pulled at the tape.

"It's too thick. You'll never break it."

Twisting to face the girl, Allison felt something gouge her thigh. "I've got scissors in my pocket that can cut the tape. Careful when you grab them. They're sharp."

Shelly dug into the pocket and pulled the scissors free.

"Don't cut yourself."

The cold steel touched Allison's arm. A tip of the blade jabbed deep into her flesh. She bit her cheek, not wanting to hinder Shelly's attempt.

"Put the tape between the blades. Make sure your hand isn't in the way. Then bring the two sides of the scissors together. Like you do when you cut paper."

The girl groaned again as she fiddled with the shears.

Guide Shelly's hands, Lord.

Slowly, she began to cut. Allison could imagine the sticky tape adhering to the sides of the scissors.

A difficult task at best, but an impossible challenge for Shelly.

Smoke filled the entryway. Shelly coughed hard.

"You have to save yourself, honey."

The tape broke, and Allison pulled her hands free.

"You did it. Good job."

She hugged Shelly, then took the shears and snipped through the tape binding her legs.

"You need to get outside."

Shelly jumped to her feet and headed to the rear of the house and the back door that led to the bramble-enclosed yard.

"You can't get through the blackberry bushes," Allison warned.

Shelly motioned her forward.

Once outside, they inhaled deep gulps of fresh air. Shelly shuffled across the lawn to the hedge.

"Careful. The thorns are sharp. You'll cut your hands."

She ducked low and shoved her full weight against a bush that gave way. A narrow path lay exposed. Shelly's hands were cut, but she'd found a way out.

"Run home, Shelly. Find Luke. Tell him to call the fire department."

She nodded, her eyes expressive.

Allison didn't want to send her off alone, but it seemed Shelly could tackle more than Allison had ever expected.

God protect her.

Confident she'd make it to safety, Allison ran back into the burning house.

Luke yelled Shelly's name as he ran through the dark woods. He came to the clearing, fearing he might find her huddled in the surrounding bushes, reliving that terrible night. He peered around the tree stumps and boulders. Finally, convinced his sister wasn't there, he raced on.

Twigs snapped. He heard the sound of something crashing through the dense underbrush. An animal or…

"Shelly," he screamed, seeing her struggle against the bushes. Her hands were bloody and scratched. Her cheeks were flushed with exertion, yet her eyes were lucid. She ran into his arms but refused his comforting embrace. Instead, she slapped his chest.

"I've been so worried about you."

She tugged on his arm, then groaned when he failed to move.

"We have to tell Bett you're all right. Plus your hands are hurt. You need to get home."

Shelly shook her head.

Fearing she was going into one of her episodes, Luke pulled her close, but she fought against his attempt.

"Shh," he soothed, causing her to become more agitated.

He patted her back, and she stiffened at his touch.

Why weren't the calming techniques working?

"All-son." The sound of her voice shocked him. She hadn't spoken since Hilary's death.

He pulled her back and stared into her eyes. "What'd you say?"

"All-son," she repeated, then pointed in the direction of the Manor.

"Does Allison need help?"

She nodded her head frantically.

Luke sniffed Shelly's hair, smelling smoke.

Bett raced into the clearing. "Oh, Shelly, come to Mama."

The girl ran into her mother's arms.

"Vic called. Someone spotted smoke coming from this direction. He wanted to ensure it wasn't our place. The fire department's on the way," said Bett.

"Allison's in trouble. I'll run ahead and see if I can help."

Please, God, let me get there in time.

* * *

Allison reentered the burning building and hit a wall of smoke that forced her to her knees. She crawled along the floor. Her lungs burned. She coughed, tried to pull in a clean breath and found only smoke.

The floor danced under her as she inched along the hallway. Would she find Craig and his father? If she didn't' hurry, she wouldn't be able to save either of them.

Blood seeped from her wrist. Too much blood. Had Shelly nicked an artery?

The stairs to the second floor creaked as flames ate through the classrooms overhead.

Her muscles ached, but she focused on moving forward.

Suddenly a deafening sound filled her ears, like a rush of wind and the crack of thunder. The house shook as a beam fell straight down through the open stairway.

Allison screamed as the massive timber crashed onto her leg, catching her in its viselike grip, the pain so intense her head spun. She gasped for air, willing herself to remain conscious.

She knew God had brought her to this point in time for a purpose. If He'd wanted her to die, He never would have sent Shelly to save her.

Allison had to hold on to hope.

But through the smoke, she saw the flames play along the top of the beam, heading straight toward her.

Hampered by flames that engulfed the front of the old school, Luke used his knife to cut a path through the ring of blackberries and charged into the burning inferno.

"Allison," he screamed, barely able to hear his own voice over the roar of the flames.

Where was she?

He fell to the floor and slapped his hands over the hardwood. He needed to keep going, despite the thick smoke and lack of visibility.

"Allison, where are you?"

He scooted forward to where a giant beam blocked the hallway.

Flames danced along the wood.

Glancing over the obstruction, he gasped. Allison lay sprawled across the floor, her leg trapped.

He pushed his weight against the giant beam. It shifted slightly. Would it be enough?

Gently, he nudged her foot free and exhaled the air he was holding in his lungs.

Raising her into his arms, he carried her from the burning building and laid her on the ground, away from the structure.

Her faint ebb and flow of breath sounded golden.

"Allison, answer me."

She blinked her eyes opened. "Luke. Where's Shelly?"

"With Bett. The fire department will be here soon."

He spied the deep nick on her wrist and the rapidly forming pool of blood. Pulling a handkerchief from his pocket, he wrapped it tightly around her wound and elevated her arm.

"Monroe and Craig are still inside," she said.

"I'm going back for them."

"What about the beam? It's blocking the hallway. You'll never make it."

"There's a root cellar on the side of the house. I'll go in that way."

She grabbed his arm. "I'm sure Monroe killed your father, Luke."

"Even more reason for me to find him. I've been eaten up with this anger too long. I couldn't live with myself if I didn't try to save him."

"No, Luke," she screamed as he pushed through the ring of bushes and headed to the root cellar.

Once again she turned to God. Would He be able to protect the man she loved?

Luke raced across the cellar and took the stairs to the first floor two at a time. At the top of the landing, he found Craig and carried him outside to safety.

Retracing his steps, Luke pushed through the thick smoke and climbed to the main floor. All around him the fire roared hot enough to sear his flesh.

Kneeling, he swept the central hallway with his hands.

On the third sweep, he made contact. Without taking time to feel for a pulse, he threw Monroe's limp body over his shoulder.

As they squeezed through the doorway to the cellar, a loud boom sounded and a section of the second floor broke free, crashing down to where the mayor had lain just seconds earlier.

Luke used care as he navigated the stairs. His lungs threatened to explode. Just in time, the smoke lifted and he saw the exit ahead.

He carried Monroe away from the house and placed him next to Craig. Then, using his knife, he expanded the path through the brambles and carried Allison to the same area.

Lightning slashed across the sky and thunder rumbled. Fat drops of rain splashed against the ground.

He knelt over Allison. Her eyes fluttered, her face deathly pale. She'd lost so much blood.

He bent close. "Stay with me, Allison."

She moaned.

"Come on, honey. You've got to hang on. For me."

But her hand went limp and her head rolled to the side.

"Allison," he screamed as the spotlight from the fire truck captured them both in its glare.

FIFTEEN

Luke stood outside the cabin two days later when the large Lincoln Continental pulled into the drive.

The driver climbed out and extended his hand. "Philip Stewart."

"Nice to meet you, sir." Luke nodded to the attractive middle-aged woman who took her place beside her husband. "Ma'am."

Bett stepped from the cabin and motioned them forward. "Y'all come in now. I'm sure you've got a lot to talk over."

Closing the cabin door behind the visitors, Bett headed for the house. "You might as well sit on the porch, Luke. I have a feeling this will take a while. Shelly's inside, acting as nervous as you are."

"Tell her to pick out a book we can read after our guests leave."

"That'll make her smile."

Luke nodded. "She's back to where she should be, Bett."

A broad grin covered his aunt's face. "Better than I'd ever expected."

He rubbed his hand over her shoulder. "A mother's love means so much."

"God gets the credit, not me."

He nodded, knowing she was right.

"The sheriff wanted to know if we'd attend services with him this Sunday," Bett said. "After all the cards and flowers from the people in town, might be nice to worship with them for a change."

"I shouldn't have made you stop your life just because I closed mine off."

"We were in this together, Luke. You remember that. I guess when you measure the amount of hurt we've had, we're kind of like Shelly, lucky to have come through it all."

Luke waited on the porch until the door to the cabin opened once again, and the doctor and his wife stepped outside.

"Thank you," Mrs. Stewart said as she dabbed a tissue at her eyes. "I'm afraid I'm too emotional to talk right now."

"We'll see you tomorrow about 4:00 p.m. for supper. Bett's been cooking up a storm."

Once they'd driven out of sight, Luke wiped his hands on his jeans and headed for the cabin. A nervous tingle tickled his palms.

He stepped inside and looked at Allison. Lying

on the couch, she was wrapped in one of his mother's quilts. Her face was still too pale.

She turned at the sound of the door closing behind him.

"How was it?" he asked.

"He asked for my forgiveness."

Luke heard the emotion in her voice.

"I never told you, but I was the one driving the night Drew died. I thought that's why my father stopped talking to me."

"But?" Luke encouraged.

"He carried even more guilt than I had. Dad was on duty in the ER the night of the accident. He felt if he'd reacted sooner or done more, Drew might have lived."

"Surely he couldn't have been expected to treat his own son."

"He called in other staff members, but even so, he held himself to blame."

"What'd you tell him?"

"How we can't close ourselves off from others. We have to hold on to hope and embrace life, pain and all. Hope leads to healing. And healing comes when we ask the Lord's forgiveness."

"How'd you get so smart?"

"I learned from you."

He took her hand and squeezed. "And you're the one who forced me back into life. I'd been holed up too long. Thanks for saving me."

"Ah, but that's what I'm supposed to say to you. Seems you saved me three times."

"We're good for each other. Why don't we hang around together for another—" he rolled his eyes and paused "—say, sixty or seventy years."

He smiled down at her. "I need you, Allison. You make life real for me, and I don't want to be without you. I know we haven't known each other long, and I'm probably getting way ahead of myself, but will you…?"

He hesitated, almost afraid to go on.

"Will I what?" she asked, a coy smile spreading across her pretty face.

"Will you marry me?"

"Yes." Allison laughed and the sound filled his heart with joy and caused him to laugh as well. Hearty, deep belly laughter that floated through the open window and brought Bett and Shelly running into the cabin.

"Everything okay?" Bett asked, her brow raised.

"Ev-thig K?" Shelly mimicked her mother.

"Couldn't be better," Luke said. "Now, why don't you give Allison that hug you've been saving up, Shelly?"

Allison held open her arms and the girl hastened forward, giggling like the happy child she was.

As the two embraced, Bett turned to Luke. "Vic wants to take Shelly and me out to dinner and to the movies in town tonight. I've got food on the stove. I thought you and Allison might like an evening alone."

Luke winked. "Why you little matchmaker. I beat you to it. Allison just said yes."

Shelly pulled out of her arms and looked from Allison to Luke. "Yes?"

"Luke asked me to marry him, honey. Would that be okay with you?"

"Grr-ate!" she said, a smile covering her face.

Bett walked to where her daughter stood and smiled down at Allison. "Did you get that phone call from your lab you've been waiting for?"

She nodded. "The board allotted additional funding for my research and asked me to be on a task force to increase awareness for both wasting disease and mad cow disease."

"Your test will ensure the safety of our blood supply," Luke said, hearing pride in his voice.

"Once I complete my research."

Bett patted Allison's hand. "We're real proud of you and grateful you solved the mystery surrounding Hilary's death. Vic said the guys from the Manor will have to stand trial. The mayor is being held for illegal drug distribution as well as his involvement with Hilary's murder and Earl's. Guess he paid the professor a huge sum of money to keep quiet, and that's how Mrs. Hightower could afford assisted living. Of course, she didn't know anything illegal was going on at the school."

Turning to Luke, Bett added, "Vic wants you to consider running for that congressional seat now that Cooper's bowed out of the race. He and his brother have a long road ahead of them with the trial and then facing whatever his illness brings."

"Winning the election would mean I'd spend time in Atlanta. Would you and Shelly be okay?"

"We can manage. Plus, Vic will be around to help. I thought maybe you'd enjoy being close to Allison while she finishes her research."

"Something going on between you and Vic?" Luke teased.

Bett smiled slyly. "He could use a good woman in his life."

"And a lit-tle Sun-shine too," Shelly added, working hard to enunciate the syllables.

Luke chucked her chin. "Sure you'll be okay without me, darlin'?"

Shelly made an *X* over on her chest. "Cross my h-art."

Mother and daughter waved goodbye as Luke stepped toward the couch where Allison rested.

"Thanks for loving me," he whispered.

"Forever and ever." She sighed as he captured her mouth with his.

* * * * *

Look for
PROTECTING HER CHILD,
the second book in the
Magnolia Medical miniseries,
available in May 2009
from Love Inspired.

Dear Reader,

I hope you enjoyed *Countdown to Death,* the first book in my Magnolia Medical series. In this story, medical technologist Allison Stewart's search for the source of a deadly disease sheds light on a cold-case crime that could shatter the peaceful life Luke Garrison has created for his handicapped sister. For both Luke and Allison, issues in the past keep them from living fully in the present, but by turning to the Lord, they are able to move beyond the pain to a place of love and acceptance. If something in your past still troubles you, I hope you'll ask the Lord to free you from that burden so you can find peace and forgiveness.

In each upcoming Magnolia Medical story, you'll meet laboratory professionals on the cutting edge of medical advances. Battling killer diseases in the laboratory, they also face human enemies who threaten them and the people they love. Watch for *Protecting Her Child,* the second book in the Magnolia Medical series, on sale in May 2009.

I love to hear from my readers. Blog with me at www.ladiesofsuspense.blogspot.com and at www.seekerville.com and visit my new Web site at www.DebbyGiusti.com.

Wishing you abundant blessings,

Debby Giusti

QUESTIONS FOR DISCUSSION

1. What initially attracted Allison to Luke and his family? Are there ways your family expresses love for one another that could be a source of hope for those around you?

2. Lack of open communication within her family increased Allison's pain over her brother's death. In your opinion, do misunderstandings always lead to alienation? Why or why not?

3. How did Cooper try to divert attention from his dysfunctional family? Who was hurt because of it? What would you have done in his situation?

4. Was Luke wrong to shelter his sister from questions the townspeople in Sterling might ask? Do you think Allison offered him sound advice concerning Shelly?

5. In what ways did Luke put his Christian faith into action? Has the outreach of someone you know touched your life and made it better?

6. John 8:32 says, "Then you will know the truth, and the truth will set you free." How does that scripture hold true for Bett?

7. What was the underlying reason Luke never searched for Hilary's killer?

8. Explain how mistakes in the past inhibited Allison and Luke from living fully in the present? What lessons could we learn from this story?

9. How does Allison's presence encourage Luke and Bett to leave their isolation and open themselves once again to love?

10. Show examples in the story that reveal how forgiveness brings healing. Can you share incidences in your own life or in the lives of those you love that illustrate the healing power of forgiveness?

11. Do you think the troubled boys should be held responsible for the actions they took when they were under the influence of medication? Why or why not?

12. How would you live your life differently if you knew you had a deadly disease that could kill you within a few years?

Widower and former soldier Evan Paterson invites his five-year-old daughter's best friend and her friend's single mother to the ranch for the holiday meal. Can these two pint-sized matchmakers show two stubborn grownups what being thankful truly means, and help them learn how to forgive and love again?

Look for

A Texas Thanksgiving

by

Margaret Daley

Available November 2008 wherever books are sold.

Steeple Hill®

Love Inspired

Twelve-year-old Jenny Walsh is worried her single dad will lose custody of her, so she begs image consultant Caitlin McBride to help with a daddy "makeover." Caitlin finds a very handsome man who's in need of a *personality* makeover, but he brushes her off—only to reappear with a heart-tugging request....

Look for

Family Treasures
by
Kathryn Springer

Available November 2008 wherever books are sold.

Steeple
Hill®

REQUEST YOUR FREE BOOKS!

2 FREE RIVETING INSPIRATIONAL NOVELS
PLUS 2 FREE MYSTERY GIFTS

YES! Please send me 2 FREE Love Inspired® Suspense novels and my 2 FREE mystery gifts (gifts are worth about $10). After receiving them, if I don't wish to receive any more books, I can return the shipping statement marked "cancel". If I don't cancel, I will receive 4 brand-new novels every month and be billed just $4.24 per book in the U.S. or $4.74 per book in Canada, plus 25¢ shipping and handling per book and applicable taxes, if any*. That's a savings of over 20% off the cover price! I understand that accepting the 2 free books and gifts places me under no obligation to buy anything. I can always return a shipment and cancel at any time. Even if I never buy another book, the two free books and gifts are mine to keep forever.

123 IDN ERXX   323 IDN ERXM

Name	(PLEASE PRINT)	
Address		Apt. #
City	State/Prov.	Zip/Postal Code

Signature (if under 18, a parent or guardian must sign)

Order online at www.LoveInspiredSuspense.com
Or mail to Steeple Hill Reader Service:

IN U.S.A.: P.O. Box 1867, Buffalo, NY 14240-1867
IN CANADA: P.O. Box 609, Fort Erie, Ontario L2A 5X3

Not valid to current subscribers of Love Inspired Suspense books.

Want to try two free books from another series?
Call 1-800-873-8635 or visit www.morefreebooks.com

* Terms and prices subject to change without notice. N.Y. residents add applicable sales tax. Canadian residents will be charged applicable provincial taxes and GST. Offer not valid in Quebec. This offer is limited to one order per household. All orders subject to approval. Credit or debit balances in a customer's account(s) may be offset by any other outstanding balance owed by or to the customer. Please allow 4 to 6 weeks for delivery. Offer available while quantities last.

Your Privacy: Steeple Hill Books is committed to protecting your privacy. Our Privacy Policy is available online at www.SteepleHill.com or upon request from the Reader Service. From time to time we make our lists of customers available to reputable third parties who may have a product or service of interest to you. If you would prefer we not share your name and address, please check here. ☐

LISUS08R

Love Inspired®
SUSPENSE

TITLES AVAILABLE NEXT MONTH

Don't miss these four stories in November

THE GOOD NEIGHBOR by Sharon Mignerey
Detective Wade Prescott has his prime suspect:
Megan Burke. He found her in the yard beside the
body of her neighbor's grandson, didn't he? Case closed.
Yet Megan's sweet demeanor has Wade believing
in her innocence. And if she is innocent, a murderer
is still at large....

THE PROTECTOR'S PROMISE by Shirlee McCoy
The Sinclair Brothers

Who could be after his widowed neighbor and
her little girl? Grayson Sinclair vows to find out—_without_
getting emotionally involved. He won't let anyone hurt
Honor Malone, or her daughter. But the threat is closer to
home than anyone realizes.

SHIELD OF REFUGE by Carol Steward
In the Line of Fire

No evidence, no other witnesses—no wonder Officer
Garrett Matthews doubts Amber Scott's claims that
she saw a kidnapping. Then someone begins tailing Amber,
and Garrett starts to suspect that she's telling the truth.
And that means that the danger she's in is real.

HOLIDAY ILLUSION by Lynette Eason
Little Paulo desperately needs a new heart. But for the
surgery, orphanage director Anna Freeman must take him
to the city she fled in fear years ago. And she finally has to
tell Dr. Lucas Freeman about her secrets. Her past. And the
danger stalking them all.

LISCNM1008